Thumbprint Mysteries

SIGN OF TERROR

BY

RICHARD FORREST

CONTEMPORARY BOOKS

a division of NTC/CONTEMPORARY PUBLISHING GROUP
Lincolnwood, Illinois USA

Thumbprint
Mysteries

MORE THUMBPRINT MYSTERIES

by Richard Forrest:

Sign of the Beast
Sign of Blood

For Pat

Cover Illustration: Troy Thomas

ISBN: 0-8092-0678-1

Published by Contemporary Books,
a division of NTC/Contemporary Publishing Group, Inc.,
4255 West Touhy Avenue,
Lincolnwood (Chicago), Illinois 60646-1975 U.S.A.
© 1999 Richard Forrest
Manufactured in the United States of America.

90 QB 0 9 8 7 6 5 4 3 2 1

CHAPTER 1

It was going to be a deadly shoot!

All the shots were directed by Orson Ordman, who nervously paced back and forth before his equipment. Ordman was a dark man of medium height with a barrel chest and large upper arms. This mildly top-heavy body combined with a slightly tipped strut created his bantam-like appearance.

He paced back and forth in front of the dozens of technicians and bystanders who surrounded Heather Mack as she stood before the Morgan Trading Post dressed in a wide hoopskirt. Three cameras would shoot simultaneously, while a bank of flood- and spotlights were adjusted to brighten the night scene. The director stopped his rooster-like prance across the front of the set and sat in a canvas chair by the center camera where he continued to shout directions in a hoarse voice.

1

Tracy Zandt, the tall, raven-haired assistant director, seemed disjointed as she picked up the director's prance in front of the Trading Post while repeating his instructions.

By day the Trading Post was a souvenir shop for tourists visiting this resort community. It was of interest to the movie crew because its two-hundred-year-old exterior was unchanged from the town's earliest days when Mohawk tribes roamed the nearby woods and hills.

Not far from the director's chair Lee Upton, a well-built blond man, focused a still camera on Heather for portrait pictures.

Behind the mass of equipment, Police Chief Ray Wilson's towering six-foot, three-hundred-pound presence dominated the crowd. The chief, along with his complete force of fifteen men, blocked streets and directed traffic away from the Trading Post so the scene would appear historically authentic. Ordinarily during this shift only three cops would be on duty. The overtime for the extra men and women was going to cost someone a pretty penny. Ray shrugged the thought away. That afternoon the mayor had requested a strong police presence and told him they were billing the movie company for the overtime plus other expenses.

The town rumor was that the cost for this thirty-second commercial topped a million and a half dollars. Everyone agreed that you didn't hire supermodel Heather Mack for minimum wage. Heather's rate for ordinary still photography modeling was over $500 an hour. The trip to Morgan with three days of night shooting and the long trip back to New York City in her private bus was going to push that wage into the high six figures.

"Can we get on with this, Orson?" Heather said to the director with tired resignation.

A makeup artist dashed in front of the cameras and

dabbed Heather's forehead with a powder puff.

Ordman pushed off his canvas chair and crossed to the center camera to peer through a viewfinder. "It's looking good, Heather. We'll do another take in a couple secs," he said as he gave instructions to two men on the lighting crew to adjust the floodlights that flanked the model.

"I really hope so," Heather said.

Orson Ordman took a final peek through the viewfinder. More than a dozen technicians, seven model-actresses, extras hired in town, and a crowd of more than a hundred onlookers were quiet while the director set up the last shot of the night.

Orson had skied on Bald Mountain near Morgan, New York, last winter. During his brief stay he had noticed the historic Morgan Trading Post on Court House Square and had filed the location away in the back of his mind. When the Breathless perfume commercial that called for a pre-Civil War setting had come into the shop, he had immediately remembered the Trading Post. Within two weeks Heather and others had been hired and the crew was on its way to the town of Morgan in the Adirondack Mountains.

This small city in upstate New York was permanent home to ten thousand people whose livelihood depended on tourists. In the summer they catered to campers and fishermen who came for the deep woods, fast streams, and clear lakes. The deer hunters arrived in the fall followed, after the first snow, by both downhill and cross-country skiers with snowmobilers cruising the spaces between.

The town nestled in a valley next to Loon Lake surrounded by pine forest at the base of Bald Mountain. Its lush surroundings of deep woods with abundant wildlife more than made up for its isolation.

A tall, slender man with broad shoulders and a wide

smile sat on the lid of a wheeled trash can on the outskirts of the crowd. Like many others in town, Diff James had been temporarily hired by the movie company. His regular job as janitor at the police services building prompted the film company to hire him to clean up after the final shoot. He arrived with his equipment of brooms and a wheeled trash can.

Diff knew he had arrived early and his work wouldn't begin for another two hours. Not only was he curious about the mechanics of filming, but being there gave him the opportunity to watch the chief's daughter, Holly Wilson.

Holly was one of several Morgan women the film company had hired as background extras. These support roles wouldn't have any lines, but they would remain in the background behind Heather and another actress. All the women on the set except the supermodel wore hooded gowns that covered everything but their faces.

Diff noticed that the director had arranged the Morgan extras in a line along the front of the Trading Post, but he had put Holly near the center of the group. Holly was placed right behind Nell Richards, another professional model, who also wore a hooded gown.

"You in the center," Ordman ordered in a raspy voice. "Take off your hood and fluff the hair."

Holly threw her hood back over her shoulders to reveal her golden-red hair.

"Hey!" Nell Richards objected. "She's only an extra and not even union. Are you telling me that I have to wear a hood while she gets a closeup?"

"I want contrast," Ordman snorted. "If you get your hair dyed red in twenty seconds, you can have the close shot. See how the babe's hair is great contrast and accents Heather's platinum blond?"

Nell Richards broke rank with the other women and walked toward Ordman. Her voice carried over the crowd. "How come you have me under a burlap sack and this redhead who's not even Actor's Equity gets the top spot?"

"Take it easy, Nell," Ordman said in a softer voice than usual. "I like the contrast in hair color. That girl, what's her name?"

"Holly Wilson," Tracy shouted.

"She doesn't have any lines like you do, so back off, all right?" His voice toughened. "Now get back on your mark so we can roll."

Nell glared at the director before she abruptly turned and stalked back to her place in line.

"Hey, Retard, how many lines you got in this big film?" Luke Laman said as his pointed boot kicked Diff's trash can. The two Laman brothers wore silver-beaded leather jackets and cowboy hats with greasy strips of ponytail hair spurting out the rear.

"They were going to give him a bunch of things to say," his brother Joe said, "until they found out Retard couldn't speak." He squeezed a soda can flat before he handed it to Diff. "You're in charge of the garbage here, right?"

"You mean Retard here can't talk?" Luke said in mock astonishment. "Well, do tell. Now how did that happen?"

"Because he's too dumb to learn how, why do you think?" Joe answered.

"Hey, bro, look at those chicks in front of the cameras. Now, me, I'd like to go partying with the one with silver hair."

"Holly, the redhead, is good enough for me," Joe said. "I like my party girls homegrown."

"Now, some in town might say that she's Retard's girl," Luke said.

"Can't be, brother. How could he ask her out since he can't talk?"

Diff slid off the can's lid and lunged toward Luke Laman, who had been expecting the attack and danced backward out of reach.

Diff's further movement was blocked by Chief Wilson, who inserted himself between the men before he put his hands on Diff's shoulders. He felt the tremors of anger surge through Diff's body. "Easy now. Don't let these two get to you."

The Laman brothers moved quickly away from the police chief and melted into the crowd.

Diff's rigid body began to relax as his tormentors left, but a deep anger that went further than responding to the brothers' remarks was still present. He felt a wide hurt because they were right. The fact of the matter was that he couldn't ask Holly out or tell her how he felt. He had decided long ago that as long as he could not speak, he would never let her know by attempting to use sign language or writing his feelings.

Ray's grip began to relax when he saw that the brothers had moved to the far side of the crowd. The danger of a fight had passed. "You calm enough now?"

Diff nodded.

"Stay away from those jokers, Diff. You know they're bad news and will ride you until they get a rise. Remember that they not only want trouble, but they come in pairs. You try to fight one and you end up taking them both on because they come as a matched set. That's exactly what they want you to do because they know that you can take one of them, but not both."

Diff wrote a quick note on the pad he always carried and handed it to Ray. The note read, 'They push me too hard and too far.'

"I know, Diff, but be patient because one of these days I am going to nail those guys. I know they're responsible for half the petty theft in Morgan, but I just haven't gotten them on anything strong enough to make them serve time." He looked toward the Trading Post where his daughter waited with the other movie extras. "Doesn't Holly look terrific out there? She's as pretty as any of those professional actresses."

Diff did not answer because he could not speak.

The director's assistant picked up a bullhorn and turned it toward the watching crowd. "All right, everyone, we are ready for a shoot," her voice boomed out over Court House Square. "We need absolute silence, so quiet on the set. Lights . . ." Floodlights blinked on as models and town extras in front of the Trading Post straightened up and assumed their assigned positions. "Camera . . . action!" the assistant director yelled over the amplifier.

Heather Mack immediately came to life when she heard "Action." Her face, which only moments before had been without animation as a mask filled with boredom, jumped vibrantly alive and consumed with zest. She moved with an animal-like grace as her hoop skirt with its several petticoats swirled around her as she walked toward the camera. She was astonishingly gorgeous.

She stopped at a foot-long piece of narrow tape placed on the walk to indicate where she should stand. "I forgot my lines," she said.

"I do not believe this! I really do not really believe anyone could be so out of it!" Orson shot to his feet and threw his clipboard directly at the actress.

Heather ducked and the clipboard bounded off Holly's nose. The redhead's eyes seemed to swirl out of focus as she fell straight forward as if poleaxed.

Diff catapulted to his feet and bounded toward the

set. Police Chief Ray Wilson grabbed Orson by the arms to bend him forward and handcuffed his hands behind his back.

Morgan's mayor's face turned ash white when he saw the movie director handcuffed by his chief of police. He sank slowly to the edge of the curb with his head in his hands.

Diff knelt by Holly, who peeked up at him with a wink. "How am I doing?" she asked in a soft whisper.

"Way to go, Orson," the assistant director said, not realizing that she still held the bullhorn at her lips. Her voice boomed out over the crowd. "You have just killed this hick town's police chief's daughter. Which means they will hang you from the courthouse. I've always told you your rotten temper would get you in big trouble one day."

The handcuffed Orson Ordman waddled over to where Holly sat with her head on Diff's lap. He knelt awkwardly because of his handcuffed hands. "Hey, Red, I really am sorry. I meant to bean old Heather over there, and I certainly didn't mean to get you." He looked up at Ray with concern. "Is the ambulance on its way? We've got to get Red here into surgery."

"Please don't ever call me Red again," Holly said. "I really hate it."

"She's alive!" Orson bellowed to the crowd. "She's alive!"

A cheer thundered from the onlookers. "This is better than a real movie," Henry Watson, the bank teller, said. He tried to revive the mayor who had slumped sideways in worry over who was going to pay the cops' overtime.

Holly leaned against Diff as if still woozy and out of focus as he helped her to stand. "He deserved it," she whispered to Diff and her father. "Grown men shouldn't lose their temper and throw things."

"Are you telling me?" Heather said when she overheard the remark. "That's why I'm divorcing the man. I just might add attempted assault along with my other court charges against you, Orson."

Ray unlocked the handcuffs on Ordman's wrists. "You do that again to anyone in Morgan and you will spend weeks in the county lockup. Do you understand me?"

Ordman glared at the huge chief of police and opened his mouth in preparation for the unleashing of a torrent of words. He paused a moment to reconsider as he looked at the gigantic man in the police uniform. His new measure made him think twice about engaging in any further verbal attacks. He swallowed twice before he spoke in a quiet and well-modulated voice. "Yes, sir. I understand. You have my word that there won't be a similar incident as long as I am in Morgan."

"All right, everyone back to your places," Tracy, the assistant director, bellowed through her bullhorn. "Showtime is over! It's back to work, kids. We have a shoot going here."

Ordman stopped next to Heather, who was going over her lines with a script girl. "My dear Heather," he said in a sweet voice that reeked of hidden anger. "Is it possible that you might try to remember all your lines for this shot? After all, there must be ten or twelve words in a row for you to memorize. Now, I realize this is difficult, but considering the money we're paying you, can we give it a go?"

"Why don't you drop dead, creep?" Heather said with a sweet smile.

"I love a happy crew," Tracy mumbled under her breath before raising her bullhorn again. "Places, everyone."

Diff left Holly with the extras and walked off the set back to his janitorial equipment. He pushed through onlookers and tried to pass Sally Way.

Until recently Sally had been a member of the Morgan Police Department where she had been employed as a communications clerk. That job had temporarily ended last week when she went on matenity leave. She refused to reveal to anyone who the father was.

"Hiya, Diff," Sally said. "I've got a secret for you." She leaned over to whisper in his ear. "You're the daddy," she said.

He shook his head violently. He knew as well as Sally it was a biological impossibility since they had never been together.

"Listen to me, Diff honey. You know it's not you and I know it's not you, but the rest of this town, including the father of that girl you really go for, is going to believe me. When they hear in no uncertain terms that you are to be a daddy, they will believe me. Get it? So you had better make the best of it and marry me before the chief gets out his shotgun to take you to our wedding. What say we set the day? How's next Saturday sound to you?"

Diff wrote a hurried note on his pad: 'I'm going to Tibet next Saturday.'

Tracy's voice again boomed over Court House Square, "All right, everyone, it's another take. Camera . . . action!"

Heather Mack came to life again. She stepped forward and walked toward her mark in front of the center camera. Three steps before she reached the spot where she was to give her lines about the virtues and terrific smell of Breathless perfume, the lights blinked out.

The cameras, floods, streetlights, and all the distant lights and signs in the area blinked out. It was a moonless night with a cloudy sky that hid the stars, so Court House Square was plunged into deep darkness.

A woman screamed.

"Don't anyone panic!" Ray Wilson's reassuring voice bellowed over the square. "This electrical grid is out, but the power plant will switch over and we'll have lights again in seconds. Everyone keep calm."

Another scream.

"Something's happening!" a man bellowed.

The electricity clicked on as the camera floods burst into light, streetlights flicked on, and store signs restarted their blinking messages.

"All right, let's get this show back on," Orson yelled at the top of his hoarse voice.

"Show back on," Tracy echoed over her bullhorn.

"Where is Heather?" Ordman asked in annoyance.

In the center of the acting area on the exact spot that contained Heather's camera mark was a hoop skirt. It sat on the walk as it someone had dropped it and simply stepped out of it.

"No more games, Heather," Ordman yelled at the crowd.

"No more games," Tracy repeated.

"Will you stop that?" Ordman ordered his assistant.

"Stop that!" Tracy echoed, followed by a quick, "Oh," and a clatter as she dropped the bullhorn.

The director paced up and down in front of the cameras. "Come out, come out, wherever you are, dearest Heather. Come on, honey," he said imploringly. "We got a bunch of people out here that we are paying a fortune by the hour. Don't hold up production any longer, babykins."

"I think you had better produce your star actress soon," Chief Wilson said.

"What do you think I'm trying to do, Chief?" Ordman

snapped. "Okay, honey, I'm sorry I got mad and threw that thing at you."

"She's gone, Orson," Tracy said. "I don't think Heather's here at all."

"Of course she's here. She's playing a practical joke on me to get even. Isn't that just like her to always be causing me trouble?"

Diff pushed through the crowd to stand next to Ray as the chief snapped a hand radio to his lips and began to establish communications with his men manning the street blocks around the square." Listen to this," he said in a voice of command. "You all know what Heather Mack looks like. God only knows her picture has recently been in the local newspaper and on TV enough times. Any of you can easily spot her, so I want a report on anyone who's seen her in the last couple of minutes. If she tries to leave the area, let me know immediately. If you've seen her since the blackout, let me know instantly. Everyone got that? Check in all posts."

Sergeant Ned Toms, who had closed Main Street west of the square, was the first cop to report in. "Toms here, Chief," he said. "That's a negative on spotting the model. We have not let anyone in or out of Main Street for the past fifteen minutes."

Diff and Ray listened as each post surrounding the square reported in with answers similar to Sergeant Toms's.

Tracy moved slowly through the crowd looking closely to see if Heather was hiding among the onlookers. "Not here," she finally called back to them.

Orson went over to Ray with a worried frown. "Something is funny here, Chief. We've checked the portable dressing rooms, she's not with the people on the square, and . . ."

"She also didn't leave the area," Ray said. "My men had all the streets closed to keep traffic away during your shoot, and she did not go in or out since we saw her last. We checked nearby buildings and they are locked up tight."

"That's impossible," Ordman said. "A woman can't just disappear in front of a hundred people."

"It would seem that she did," Ray answered.

Diff wrote a single word on his pad and handed it to Ray. 'Sewers,' it said.

CHAPTER 2

Diff James was slowly lowered into the sewer through the manhole at the foot of Court House Square. A heavy rope was tied to his feet and he held long police flashlights in each hand as he slowly went down into the dank cave-like chamber. The swaying lights created strange shadows that slipped and slid along old brick walls.

"Man, I wouldn't do that for ten thousand dollars," a voice echoed into the sewer from above.

Diff directed the lights straight down the deep sewer running under the square. This part of the town's system was one of the oldest and had been built over a hundred years ago. It was dug and bricked deep and wide to take large amounts of mountain runoff water from early spring floods. When Diff had nearly reached the bottom of the sewer, he signaled to his surface handlers by scissoring his feet rapidly.

Ray had asked him to make the trip into the deep sewer not because he didn't like Diff, nor did he feel that this man who could not speak was any braver than other men who worked for him. He asked Diff because there was no argument in the town of Morgan and the county of Mohawk that Diff James was by far the best woodsman and tracker in this part of the state. If there was anything to be discovered under the square, Diff would see it.

It had been a dry summer and little rain had fallen for several weeks. The sewer was empty and the layer of silt at the bottom had dried to a thick sludge. There were no human footprints in the floor of silt. The only tracks were the ones he expected to find of the rats that he knew lived down here by the thousands.

He gave the signal to be pulled up.

Without warning, the ropes holding him went slack and he plummeted into the dank stink at the bottom of the sewer chamber. He managed to twist during the last few feet of fall so that he landed in the muck on his side rather than head down. The impact of the fall knocked the lights from his fingers as he hit the caked mud with a force that knocked his wind out.

He heaved with gasping struggles for breath.

Hidden rats took his painful wheezes as a signal to emerge from their hiding places in the drains that led into the main holding tank. They scurried over his body, making sharp, painful nips to his hands and feet as other tiny teeth tore through the cloth of his pants into his thighs and shins. If he could, Diff would have screamed in pain.

"What's happening down there? Who did that? Who let that rope go?" Ray demanded on the surface.

"Sorry about that, Chief," Luke Laman said. "That dumb rope just slipped out of our hands and we just couldn't help it."

"I swear to God you two boys will pay for that," Ray thundered.

As his breathing returned to normal, Diff scrambled to his feet, his shoes sinking deep into the sludge beneath the street. Rats ran up his body and over his head as he snorted and knocked them away with his hands. Not far from him he saw one of the flashlights, base down in the sludge with its light pointed toward the roof. He reached toward its glow as more rats scampered over his outstretched arm.

"Hold on, Diff. I'm coming!" was the slow, easy drawl of Sergeant Ned Toms. There was a reassuring quality to the man's voice that helped calm the mounting terror caused by the scampering rodents. Diff stiffened and turned the flashlight up toward the open manhole. He saw Toms, with his rope in a mountain climber's sling, slide down toward him with a spare line wrapped around his arm.

Diff knew that Toms was the leader of the Mountain Rescue team and was an accomplished mountaineer and trained paramedic. If anyone could get him out of this mess quickly, this was the man to do it.

Sergeant Toms reached Diff and slapped the spare rope into his arms. "Oh," Toms groaned as the rats turned their attack toward him. "Pull us up!" he yelled to the surface. "For God's sake, get us both out of here!" He was already rising before he finished.

Diff wrapped the line under his shoulders and around his buttocks as it tightened and raised him toward the surface.

As Diff's head came through the open manhole, Ray reached down to pull him up the rest of the way. "Are you okay?"

Diff nodded.

"See anything down there?" Ray asked after he

realized that Diff had not suffered any permanent or serious damage. While he talked, Ned Toms began to apply antiseptic and small bandages over the rat nips.

Diff shook his head.

Ray looked deeply puzzled. "This whole thing doesn't make one bit of sense. How could a woman disappear into thin air in front of a hundred people? How long were the lights out?" he asked no one in particular.

"I'd say about ten seconds," Sergeant Ned Toms said in his measured drawl. The crowd murmured agreement. "You got to get a tetanus booster shot, Diff. It had better be as soon as possible because those rats are filthy beasts."

Ray continued with his thoughts as if speaking to himself, "The streets were blocked off, and we know no one left the square. Now you tell me that no one is underneath the street. The surrounding buildings have been completely checked and they are all locked and no one has broken into any of them. People," Ray continued, "we have one hell of a mystery on our hands."

The flames of anger building up in Orson Ordman forced him to yell in Ray's face. "I want action, do you hear me? I want the National Guard called in, the sheriff's department alerted, and a posse formed to find my star!"

"As far as we know, nothing has happened to her," Ray answered.

"Are you crazy?" Orson's face turned a deep shade of red. "She disappeared during the few seconds the lights were out. I have a crew waiting to finish this film and she's not here. We can't go on without her."

"That is your problem and not a police matter," Ray answered.

"A crime has been committed and I demand action!"

"I admit it's a mystery, but all we know is that a lady

has disappeared, and we can't even put out a missing persons alert until she's been gone twenty-four hours."

"Twenty-four hours! Do you realize how much that will cost me? I have a union crew up here from the city, and they get paid high rates not including room and board and other items we have to pay for. So listen, you hick cop, get on the stick! If you can't do it, get me someone who can."

"You are out of order, Mr. Ordman," Ray answered in a level, authoritative voice that Diff recognized. This tone sprang from a deep anger within the chief that he was fighting to control.

"You stupid hick!" Orson Ordman's fist lashed out toward Ray's chin.

Ray Wilson's hand leaped out and caught the fist in midair. Slowly his massive fingers closed tightly over Ordman's hand. Without any change of expression, the tendons on Ray's arm stood out in bold relief as he squeezed.

"Hey, man, stop it! You're crushing my fingers."

"You just assaulted a police officer," Ray said.

"Sorry, okay? I'm sorry. Let me go, all right? We'll talk in twenty-four hours if Heather's still gone. Right?"

Diff had a feeling that Heather was going to be gone a lot longer that one day. He had a sense she might be gone forever.

Sergeant Toms's hand closed gently over his shoulder. "Time we both got that tetanus booster shot, Diff," the police officer said. "Come on, we'll drive over to the hospital in my car."

Ray Wilson watched them cross the square and climb into a Morgan police cruiser. He had affection for both men for different reasons. Ned Toms was his right arm, the officer he could always count on to keep a level head. The sergeant always thought before he spoke and did his work to the best of his ability without being asked. He was a huge asset to the police force and the small city of Morgan with its limited number of officers.

His feelings for Diff came from a different source and for far different reasons. Perhaps it was because the mute man was so different from Ned Toms. Diff had arrived in Morgan one dawn eleven years ago. He had wandered into town wearing torn clothing without shoes and seemed dazed and confused.

The police had been called and Ray had been the first to arrive on the scene to find a cab driver trying to talk with the confused young man. Ray had quickly determined that the newcomer was mute, was very hungry, and had recently been though a very difficult experience. Where he came from and even his real name were somehow lost in this stranger's fog of confusion.

It had taken them years to find out where Diff came from and what horrible events made him unable to speak. Although they finally discovered the emotional cause of his difficulty, it had not been enough to allow Diff to regain his speech.

Ray had taken the responsibility of caring for Diff. He had fixed an apartment over his garage, while Holly had taught the man who could not speak how to read, eat with proper utensils, and a great many other ordinary things that he seemed not to know. Ray had also obtained the janitorial job at the police station for Diff. The chief had been astonished not only at the man's ability to learn police methods, but also his knowledge of animals and wood lore.

Ray knew that if Diff could speak, he would offer Diff a position as a uniformed member of the force and that Diff would probably accept. If Diff could speak, perhaps he and Holly . . . But those things would never come to pass since not one word had passed Diff James's lips since his arrival in Morgan.

*   *   *

It was a day later while Diff was washing the windows in the chief's office that Orson Ordman appeared in the doorway. Ray looked at the impatient movie director and tented his fingers before he spoke. "What can we do for you today, Mr. Ordman?"

"Well, if it doesn't interfere with your busy schedule, it might be nice if you could attempt to locate one of this country's supermodels, Heather Mack. Somehow or other she still seems to be missing."

"The proper time has now elapsed for you to make a formal missing persons application," Ray said.

"If it isn't too much trouble, sir."

Diff could see the director's tight face reflected in the glass of the window he was washing. It didn't take a great deal of psychology to realize that the man's present polite attitude was only surface deep, and that he still considered Ray Wilson a small-town hick cop.

"Of course, Mr. Ordman. What you request can be arranged," Ray answered in a voice that out-phonied Ordman's. In this act of extreme politeness, both men were obviously on to each other and aware of their real attitudes, but the game of manners continued. "Please come in and sit down so that I can obtain the necessary information from you."

Orson approached the chair in front of the chief's desk very carefully as if he expected the large cop to lunge across the furniture after him. He slowly sat down and cleared his throat while Ray made several entries on a police form and handed it across the desk to the director.

Orson completed the information on the form and

handed it back. "My assistant and I have called New York City and talked to several of Heather's friends, people in her apartment building, and her modeling agency. No one has seen or heard from her since she came to Morgan."

"We will put an all points bulletin out to all police agencies in the state in addition to our search of the complete town and surrounding area. The sheriff and his deputies will make a similar search in the county."

"There's enough woods and lakes around here to hide an army. If she's been taken off somewhere . . ."

"One of our employees is a highly skilled tracker," Ray said.

"Oh, who's that?"

Ray pointed a thumb over his shoulder toward where Diff was washing windows. "Diff James is the best I've ever seen. No one in this county beats his knowledge of the woods."

"A window cleaner?" Orson Ordman said in astonishment. "Isn't that the same guy who was dumb enough to go down in that sewer?" He stood up to lean over the desk as a red flush rose from his neck. His false manners immediately disappeared as his temper flared until it burst to the surface. "You have got to be kidding! Do you have it in for me or something, Chief?"

"He's the best man I've got for this type of job. If Heather Mack is in or around the town of Morgan, Diff will find her."

"I can't believe what I'm hearing. A hick cop is telling me that he's going to find Heather by sending his janitor out to look for her. Now I've heard everything!"

When Ray stood, his commanding height seemed to awe the director into taking several backward steps. "I think we have all the information we need from you, Mr. Ordman. Now get out of my office."

"Okay, I'm going, so there's no need to get mad. I just wondered about your staffing, that's all." He opened the door and was about to step into the hall when Ray snapped a question at him.

"I understand you were once married to Heather Mack?" Ray asked.

"Actually, I still am," Orson slowly replied in a guarded manner. "The divorce isn't final because of some legal arguments over dividing our money."

"Is that right?" Ray said. "In that case, then, her disappearance is very convenient for you, isn't it?"

"I resent that, Chief. It's true our lawyers are arguing back and forth, but I still thought enough of her to hire her for this shoot."

"So you did, Mr. Ordman," Ray said. "So you did."

*   *   *

That night Ray crossed his backyard and came up the stairs to Diff's apartment over the garage. He carried a map of Mohawk County which he spread over the kitchen table.

"I've divided the area around Morgan into squares of a hundred square yards. I've hired a temp worker to do the janitor thing at the station while you're assigned full time to the search until you've checked off every square on this map."

Diff wrote a note that said, 'I'll need some items of Heather's personal clothing for the dog to smell.'

"Figured you would," Ray said. "I've got a box of her things at the house that we picked up from the portable dressing room. I'd like you to get started at first light in the morning."

*   *   *

Bushy was the unlikeliest tracking dog in all of New

York State and perhaps in the nation. His size immediately took him out of the ordinary hunting dog category since working field dogs do not ordinarily weigh over two hundred pounds and stand six-foot-six when they place their paws on your shoulders.

In addition to size, the animal's mixed ancestry consisted of part German shepherd mixed with a bit of Saint Bernard, topped off with a little Newfoundland for good measure. Although the huge dog ordinarily worked as a guard dog at the Morgan Airport, his relationship with Diff had grown over the past year. Man and animal seemed to have a developed a deep understanding like many dogs and masters so that spoken words were not necessary and responses were more important than speech.

As a member of the Mountain Rescue Team, Diff had not only learned mountaineering, rescue techniques, and survival skills, he had also been assigned by its leader, Ned Toms, to obtain a rescue tracking dog. Somehow tracking with Bushy seemed to work and the airport manager, grateful for past favors, had been pleased to loan the animal to Diff and the rescue team whenever necessary.

At six A.M. Diff picked up the dog at Morgan Airport and drove back to Court House Square. He parked his pickup in front of the Trading Post where the filming had taken place the night Heather disappeared. He would began his search here and work out into the other map grids in circular fashion.

With Bushy on a short leash they started around the square and worked their way up Main Street past the police station and continued on, searching the squares leading to the far edge of town. When they reached the city limits, they began to work the squares to the north and then backtracked toward the main part of town.

They worked at a fast walking pace with the dog's head held high as he attempted to pick up Heather's scent. If and when Bushy had a "hit," he would stop in front of a house, building, or wooded place to indicate to Diff that the scent was strong in that area.

In two days' time they had covered most of the town and a half mile on either side with only a few slivers of map-grid squares on the western part remaining. Diff knew from Ray's nightly reports that sheriff's deputies were covering large chunks of the county, while forest rangers were alerted to look in the nearby forests and mountains.

Bushy trotted happily by his side, glad for the freedom of the long walks away from the confines of the fenced area he patrolled at the airport. The dog did not exhibit any sign of a "scent hit" until noon of the third day when they approached the gates of the old Morgan Cemetery.

The dog stopped stock still by the iron picket fence that ran around the perimeter of the closed graveyard. The animal's body tensed as he stiffened with a low growl that issued from the depths of his throat. This was the signal he had been trained to give when he wanted to signal Diff to a "hit."

In the cemetery? Diff wanted to ask. *Do you really think you smell something in the graveyard?*

The dog remained rigid, which answered Diff's unspoken questions. He pushed against the rusting gate until it slowly squeaked open wide enough for man and dog to enter into the old cemetery. They walked along an overgrown stone path that led through the center of the graveyard.

They walked slowly along the path, past lines of weathered headstones on one side and rows of stone crypts on the other.

In the distance ahead, a figure ran from one side of the path to the other before it disappeared behind a crypt.

Diff was startled as the dog by his side growled and assumed an attack position.

Twenty yards away, the figure ran back across the stone path and disappeared behind a line of gravestones. Diff realized that what he had first thought was dark clothing because of the glare of the sun was really army camouflage fatigues.

He wished he had taken Ray's advice and accepted a police officer escort or at least carried a shotgun. The dog by his side growled again and he realized that he did have a powerful weapon in Bushy. *Okay, boy, it's up to you,* Diff thought. *I can't yell out to whoever that is, so you're going to have to get him.* He unleashed the dog.

Bushy sprang forward without need of command and raced down the stone path until he made a right angle turn into a line of tombstones.

"Help! A hound from hell!"

Diff followed the dog's route until he found that Bushy had cornered the man dressed in army clothing against one of the graves. The man's back was pressed against a headstone while his hands waved frantically in front of his face in an attempt to keep the growling dog away.

"Don't let him get me!"

Diff recognized the man dressed in fatigues as Corry. He was a very tall man who was so rail thin that the children in town sometimes ran after him calling out, "Corry, Corry, Skeleton Corry." The grocery cart parked farther up the path in front of a tomb was filled with clothing and a jumble of other objects that proved the dog had cornered the town of Morgan's only homeless person.

Corry—for he had no other name—slept under bridges, in abandoned barns, in vacant homes, or any other place he could find. He never slept in the same place two nights in a row and during the day was always on the move. He was often seen pushing the grocery cart with his few possessions in front of him as he walked sadly through town looking for that night's lodging.

Corry gestured toward a crypt on the other side of the walk near his cart. "I wasn't hurting anyone. Did you kill her?"

Diff wrote a note on his pad as quickly as he could. 'Kill who? Show me where.'

"Don't know who she is," Corry said. "But I found one of those grave houses open and I went inside to make a place to sleep tonight. When the door opened and the light fell over the coffin, I saw her."

Another note. 'Show me.'

"Leash the dog. Okay?"

Diff put Bushy back on the leash and the dog, sensing that all was well, quieted down.

"Follow me," Corry said as he slowly walked toward where his cart was parked.

Diff and the dog followed the man in the loose-fitting clothes down the line of headstones and crypts until he stopped before one that was built to look like a model of the Lincoln Memorial. The heavy door was open and Diff walked inside as Bushy signaled a "hit."

The platinum-haired Heather Mack, wearing a short skirt and peasant blouse, was stretched out on top of a stone coffin with her arms folded over her chest.

Diff knew she was not asleep.

CHAPTER 3

The old Morgan Cemetery was surrounded by cars and trucks of every description. A line of sheriff's deputies, requested by Chief Ray Wilson, moved in a search line across the grave plots. Each deputy walked two feet from the man by his side with downcast eyes looking for any clue that might help solve the murder of the dead model.

Two of Ray's uniformed police stood guard at the crypt where the body had been discovered by Diff and Corry. The medical examiner with a police photographer were inside the vault examining and photographing the body. Outside the tomb Ray paced up and down with body language that indicated his nervous tension.

"A TV crew from Albany wants to film inside the vault," Sergeant Ned Toms said in his quiet way.

"Nope," Ray answered. "Tell them no way because the

M.E. is still inside with the body. Don't those jokers have any respect for the dead?"

"They don't seem to, sir," Toms answered.

"How about the lab guys I asked the state police to send up here?" Ray snapped.

"On their way." He looked down at his wristwatch. "They should be here anytime now," Toms answered in his same level voice. "If they can't get inside with the body, the TV people would like an interview with you. If you won't let them in the murder scene right now, they'd like to film inside the vault after the body is gone. They tell me this is a big story, and they'd really like to make the six o'clock network news."

"Tell them we'll let them have a quick shoot after the lab people do their thing in there," Ray said. "You!" he said as he pointed his finger at Corry, who was sitting on a headstone next to Diff. "Come here and tell me again how you found her."

Corry shot to his feet and turned to run down the stone path until Diff put his hand tightly on the homeless man's shoulder and shook his head. He led him over to where Ray and Ned Toms stood.

"Okay, Corry," Ray said. "Run it by me again as to how you just happened to walk into this particular crypt which just happened to contain the body of Heather Mack."

"Sleep," Corry said.

"What's that supposed to mean?" Ray snapped back.

"He sleeps in a different place each night," Toms said as he acted as interpreter for the man of few words. "Every day he takes everything he owns around in that grocery cart while he looks for a place to sleep that night. Since Morgan isn't the biggest city in the world, he's running out of different places to sleep. I guess he was really getting desperate if he was trying the cemetery."

"Why this particular crypt, Corry?" Ray questioned.

"It was open," was the homeless man's brief reply.

"He means he walked through here and saw that the iron gate across the vault entrance was slightly ajar. He decided to go inside and that's when he found the body," Toms added to Corry's short statement.

"How about maybe it came down like this?" Ray said. "You're walking through the cemetery looking for a place to sleep or maybe some deposit bottles to pick up, and bang! You see one of the most beautiful women in the country sitting all alone on a headstone. You make a move on her, but she resists, maybe screams and threatens cops, so you kill her to keep her quiet."

The homeless man looked confused until he finally shook his head as he fought for the words to answer. "Don't remember."

"He blacked out maybe," Toms added.

"You killed her but can't remember it. Right, Corry?" Ray pressed.

"How'd I do it?" Corry said, trying to be as agreeable as possible.

"Well, let's just say you . . ." Ray turned to call through the crypt's open door. "Hey, Doc, how did she die?"

"Single gunshot in the head," a voice called back from inside with words that echoed out of the stone vault and across the cemetery. The line of searchers stopped and turned toward the sound, while onlookers and newspeople held back behind the fence gave a collective gasp.

Corry's "No" was more like a grunt.

"You were in the army. You can shoot." Ray snapped.

The homeless man began to realize the seriousness of

his situation and twinges of fear entered his brief responses. "No money," he was finally able to get out.

Sergeant Toms translated this by saying, "Corry doesn't think he shot her, Chief. If he had a gun, he would have sold it a long time ago to buy food."

Ray shook his head in agreement. "I guess you would have, Corry. I guess you would have."

"Come on with me, Corry," Sergeant Toms said as he led the homeless man away from the crypt. "I think it's time for your yearly checkup at the hospital."

The homeless man shook his head in agreement and managed, "Guess so, Sarge. I coulda' sworn I saw a dead body in that place. But you know, this is a cemetery. Where else would you expect to find dead bodies?"

"You've got something there, Corry," Toms said as he pushed the grocery cart of possessions toward another police cruiser where it was taken by another cop. "Longest sentence I ever heard you say."

"My stuff?" Corry said as he stubbornly stopped in the center of the stone path and pointed to where his possessions were being loaded into the trunk of the other cruiser.

"For the time being all your possessions are evidence, Corry," Ned said. "You'll get it all back as soon as they're finished with them and you're out of the hospital." The homeless man seemed determined not to leave without the remainder of his things, but an even more stubborn Ned Toms led him firmly to the police cruiser.

"You know," Ray said to Diff, "I worry about that guy all winter long because I'm always afraid he's going to freeze to death. I have the men on patrol keep an eye open for him. On the coldest nights we bring him to the station and let him sleep in one of the holding cells."

Diff nodded in agreement as he remembered last winter's cold spell when it hovered around ten degrees below zero for over a week. One morning on his way to work, he had seen Corry pushing his cart along Main Street while shivering nearly uncontrollably in his army field jacket. Diff had spent two hundred of his hard-earned dollars to buy Corry a good mountain sleeping bag, and in addition he gave the homeless man one of his own down jackets.

Diff felt an odd attachment to this man without a home because both men had a past that confused them in different but unhappy ways. A life history made one a wanderer who must sleep in a different place each night. The other had given up his voice as a young child when he could not cry out to express his hurt.

Doctor Lars Sikes, the assistant medical examiner for Mohawk County, came out of the crypt carrying his medical bag. "Okay, Ray, I've done my thing with her for now so it's okay to have the ambulance crew take her away."

"What information do you have for us, Doc?" Ray asked.

"She's dead," was the reply.

"I know that! What can you add to that?"

"A single gunshot wound to the head. The weapon fired a small caliber bullet which caused an entry wound at the rear of the head. There's no exit wound so I suspect I'll find the shell when I do the autopsy."

"That sounds like a gangland killing," Ray said.

"Who knows?" the M.E. said with a scowl as he started down the stone path toward his car.

"Hey! What about the time of death?" Ray called after him.

"Prelim estimate is at least three days," the doctor said without turning.

"That would be about the time she disappeared from the filming."

"Suspect it was about then or shortly thereafter," the doctor said as he reached his car and climbed in.

Ray turned to Diff. "It seems like we have a mystery on our hands, Diff. A beautiful model disappears in front of dozens of technicians and police without a trace when the lights go off for a few seconds. Days later her body is found a mile away inside a tomb. Figure that one out for me!"

*   *   *

Holly Wilson sat at the dressing table in her upstairs bedroom brushing her hair as the pickup turned in the drive. Diff parked the truck and walked quickly toward the steps that led up to his small apartment over the garage.

The hairbrush fell to her lap as she watched Diff take the steps two at a time with an animal-like grace. The muscles in his back moved in marked rhythm under his snow-white T-shirt. She knew that if he were turned toward her to come down the steps he might look at her across the backyard and smile. She loved his smile, the way he looked, and his attitude toward life. In fact, she was . . . She picked up the brush and began to do her hair again with strong strokes that made her wince in pain.

Years ago when her father had found Diff wandering the streets and brought him home to be taken care of, they had done a great deal for him. The house had been lonely since her mother died, and it was nice to have another person besides her father on the property. It would have been even better if he could speak and they could talk together.

They now knew why he could not speak. They had

discovered the reason last year when they had finally been able to locate the town near where he had been born and raised. Diff had been the only child of an older couple who lived on a remote and isolated farm on the outskirts of Waycross, a town the size of Morgan thirty miles away.

His father fell into a deep depression when his wife died. This seemed to cause confused thinking that convinced him the devil had taken possession of Diff. He had nearly beaten the boy to death, but had stopped at the last moment and thrown the child into an ice cellar underneath the barn.

Diff grew up in that cellar prison, fed only what scraps of food his father threw into the hole. He had finally tunneled out under the barn, and at night near dawn would run in the nearby woods to search for food. It was during these times that he established his knowledge of the woods and its animals.

It was also during those years that the abused adolescent had lost his ability to speak, and since his arrival in Morgan he had not uttered a word.

The medical and psychological tests that Ray arranged were not able to locate any physical reason for his lack of speech. His accomplishments proved that Diff was of more than average intelligence since he was able to learn to write and was a constant reader of books. He knew the woods and a great many other things, but he still could not speak.

Holly, who was a sign language teacher at the nearby school for the deaf, had taught Diff to sign. It wasn't that his hearing was poor—in fact, it was quite acute. However, his ability to sign meant that he could sometimes talk with Holly without the constant need to write notes.

Holly sighed as she continued brushing. It would seem that some things were just not to be.

*   *   *

Since the janitor and chief of police worked the same hours, Ray and Diff often rode to work together. They left the house at the top of the hill and drove toward Court House Square and the police station which was several blocks farther down Main Street.

"All right, everyone, take your places!" Tracy Zandt's voice boomed out as they approached the square.

"Oh, boy," Ray said. "I think something is happening down there." He speeded up until they made the last turn that entered into the square, where he was forced to jam on the brakes. A sawhorse manned by three uniformed guards blocked the street.

"What's going on here?" Ray yelled. "That thing's blocking the road. Get it down immediately!"

"Hey, Kelly!" one of the guards yelled over to a supervisor half a block away. "The local honcho is ticked off!"

The supervisor ambled over to Ray's cruiser and saluted. "Good morning, Chief. Top of the day to you," he said cheerily.

"Morning, Kelly," Ray said. "And what brings the hospital security officer down to the square to block my streets?"

"We have permission from the mayor, Chief," Kelly said. "We have orders to keep all traffic away from the movie people. The director said he wanted no more town police, so the movie company hired me and I brought in private guards from Waycross."

"Why wasn't I informed?" Ray said as he slammed from the car and marched toward the Trading Post where lights and cameras were set up once again for a filming.

Diff moved over to the driver's seat and parked the cruiser at a bus stop since obviously no buses were going through the square this morning. He ran after Ray to catch up with the angry chief.

Except for the time of day, everything else seemed similar to the way it was the night Heather Mack had disappeared. Crowds of curious onlookers surrounded the front of the Trading Post where actors were lined up in front of the cameras. Holly, who wore a period costume without a hood so that her gold-red hair fell over her shoulders, stood in the forefront of the hired extras.

Orson Ordman paced back and forth in front of the lights and cameras with his assistant, Tracy Zandt, a few steps behind.

Ray pushed past the assistant cameraman who tried to keep him off the set. "Have you no feelings?" he yelled at Ordman. "You've started filming again the day after your star was found dead. I'd like to know who gave permission for a gathering like this and the closing of the streets. Those are police matters that require authorizations for permits."

Ordman turned from giving instructions to glare at Ray. "Let me tell you something, Chief. We're all sorry that Heather is gone, but we can't help her now. We have a film to make, and we've already spent a small fortune without a foot of usable film, so we have to press on. I have permission from the Breathless perfume people to change the script from a night to a day scene. As for what I'm doing here, why don't you ask your mayor who's standing right over there?" He pointed to the side of the set where Mayor Will Randall stood smiling as he held the hands of a blond actress.

The mayor gave Ray a mildly embarrassed grin and

said, "Permission granted," as the blond kissed his cheek. "Permission granted again," he said again as the actress repeated the action.

"Well, I'll be . . ." Ray said in complete surprise.

Diff knew exactly why Ray was surprised. Mayor Randall was a tall, thin man who always looked worried. They were never sure whether this worry was due to the problems the town faced or because of his fear of his wife who absolutely terrified him. It was perhaps more than chance that the smiling mayor holding the hands of a lovely actress had a wife who was now visiting relatives in Chicago.

"I think we know how permission was granted on this deal," Ray said to Diff out of the corner of his mouth.

With great reluctance, Randall waved good-bye to the actress, who took her place on the set before he scurried over to Diff and Ray. "No problems here, Chief," he said. "The movie company is paying the town for cleanup and any other costs. They have hired their own security police, so we won't have to bring in your people for overtime."

"He didn't even wait until the body was cold," Ray said. "And at one time the dead woman was his wife."

"Actually she still was," Tracy Zandt said. "They were legally separated, but they were having a knockdown legal battle over dividing the money."

"How can they film with Heather dead?" Ray asked.

Tracy waved toward the center of the set where an actress wearing a hoop skirt was at the exact position Heather occupied when she disappeared. "That's Nell Richards," the assistant said. "She's taking Heather's place."

"Why the big rush on all this?" Ray asked.

"Orson has a contract with the perfume people. Now

that Heather is officially dead, the insurance company will pay for her replacement and the money lost because of her unfinished film."

"Then Orson actually benefits by Heather's death?" Ray said.

"Yes, as a matter of fact I do," Orson said as he walked over to them. "Not only did the insurance money pay cancellation costs due to her death, but the court battle we were having is now over." Without waiting for an answer he strode back to his actors lined up in front of the Trading Post.

"I can't believe the man's star and wife is found dead one day and he's doing business as usual a day later," Ray said.

"I do not believe this!" Orson Ordman screamed in a fit of temper. He kicked over a floodlight whose glass front broke with a loud crash.

"Fix that lamp!" Tracy screamed at the lighting crew. "Get me a replacement immediately!"

"Can't you people remember your places for all of ten seconds?" Orson said. "Get back to where you belong!" he yelled with a stomp of his foot like a small child.

"This guy is thirty-two years old going on five," Ray said to Diff.

The actors rearranged themselves slightly in the hope a new pattern would stop the director's tantrum.

"I am on my spot," Nell Richards, who had taken Heather's place, announced.

"Nell, baby, you are not the star you think you are yet, so don't tell the director what to do," Orson said. He moved her two feet to the left. "Now try and get your little, teeny, tiny brain to remember this spot. Or should we paint a big red X on the ground for you to stand on?"

"Am I in the right spot?" Holly asked with a smile.

Ordman's manner instantly changed as he put his arm around Holly's waist. "My dear, Red Babykins, wherever you are is the right spot."

"What's with this Babykins stuff? He'd better get his hands off her. He doesn't know who he's dealing with. This guy isn't for real," Ray said.

Too real for me, Diff thought.

CHAPTER 4

Diff could tell by the way Ray rushed out the door, jumped into his cruiser, and burned rubber as he scrambled down the drive that something was wrong at the big house. He was hardly out of sight when a Jaguar slowly turned into the drive and slowed to a stop.

Orson Ordman leaped from the sports car to rush to the passenger side to open the door for Holly. He executed a gallant bow which caused her to laugh merrily as he offered his arm to escort her to the side porch. Their faces tilted closely together as they talked in low tones for a few moments in the doorway, but they were too far away for Diff to hear the words. After a few minutes Holly opened the door and gestured for Orson to follow her inside.

What were they doing in there?

Vivid mental pictures that he didn't care for flashed

before him like rapid movie scenes. Each image his mind created was worse than the one before. He imagined them stepping into the living room that ran the length of the front of the house. He had a clear mental picture of Orson folding Holly into his arms and holding her tightly as she looked up at him with love before they began to kiss.

The necking scene quickly faded to be replaced by another one even worse. They were sitting on the couch holding hands as the movie director talked with great animation. He was a bright man who, when he didn't lose his temper, could talk the pants off the devil with either funny stories or more serious topics. Tonight would start with funny stories that would pour forth like a waterfall of warmth. Holly would laugh at his zany anecdotes as he recounted the wild life lived in the movie colonies of the world. Then his voice would drop and the laughter would stop as he became quite serious to tell her how beautiful she was and that she too could be the supermodel to replace the departed Heather Mack.

Diff wanted to sneak down the stairs and slither across the yard like a furtive animal until he was able to peer in the dining room window toward the living room couch. He wanted to spy on them until he couldn't stand it any longer and was forced to pick up a large rock and throw it though the window directly at the brainy director's talking head.

He would have been ashamed of his secret thoughts if they hadn't been so ridiculous that they made him want to laugh—if he could. He forced himself to turn from the window and begin to wash his few dinner dishes. He broke a cup and a glass in the process.

It was half an hour later before Diff heard the purr of the powerful engine and watched the Jaguar pull out of the drive. He saw Holly standing on the porch waving good-bye.

The Jag had hardly turned the corner before Ray's police cruiser turned into the drive and drove to the end of the pavement where it turned sideways in front of Diff's apartment. It was followed by several county sheriff cars and a couple of Morgan cruisers. Doors burst open as cops and deputies jumped from their cars in crouched positions and filled the yard in a semicircle around the garage. Three men from the sheriff's department carried assault rifles and wore body armor as they fanned out across the yard and took up firing positions with their weapons pointed up toward Diff's apartment.

"You are out of your living mind!" Ray Wilson yelled at Sheriff Big Red Downs.

"Get out of the way, Chief," the sheriff who was even larger than Ray yelled back. "We're taking the mute in."

"Over my dead body!" Ray snapped back as he stood in front of the narrow stairs that led up to the apartment.

"Maybe it can be arranged that you be busted for aiding a criminal," Sheriff Downs snapped.

"He is not one of the bad guys and you know it," Ray said. "And you can't arrest me in my own town."

"You want me to give it a try?"

The screen door slammed as Holly, wearing a flowered apron, ran into the yard. "What in the world is going on here? You men look like you're ready for a world war."

"We're taking a killer in, miss," Sheriff Downs said.

"They are trying to arrest Diff," Ray said. "Have you ever heard of anything so stupid?"

"Check the back of the place," Downs yelled. "There's enough noise out here to wake the dead. Maybe the guy can't speak, but he can sure hear all right so now he knows we're here."

"What in the world is he talking about?" Holly said in alarm.

"We have strong evidence, Miss Wilson," Sheriff Downs said. "Evidence that your father chooses to ignore, but which the district attorney does not. A warrant has been issued for Diff James's arrest based on that evidence, and I have been instructed to bring him in."

"What evidence?" Holly asked.

"No time for that now," Downs said as he cupped his hands around his mouth and called up to Diff. "All right, we know you're up there! Come down the stairs slowly with your hands high in the air. You hear me, James? You had better answer me right now this minute."

"I would like to remind you, Downs, that Diff cannot talk," Ray said.

"Okay, yeah, you're right," the sheriff replied. "Get down here now, James!"

Diff raised his hands above his head and slowly walked out the door and down the steps to the waiting squad of police. There were nearly a dozen people in the backyard with drawn weapons, but the only thing he saw was the stricken look on Holly's face.

*   *   *

They handcuffed him to a wooden straight chair in a bare office at the sheriff's building. The room was built for police interviews so it had no windows, two wooden straight chairs, a long table in the center of the room, and a mirror that ran the length of one wall.

Diff knew that when things calmed down, they would take turns questioning him. Right now the room was crowded with Sheriff Downs, three deputies, and Sergeant Ned Toms, and in the far back of the room Police Chief Ray Wilson leaned against the wall with a very concerned look.

"Everyone out of here except for Deputy Marvel," the sheriff's voice boomed.

Everyone except a single deputy and Ray still standing against the wall quickly filed out. The sheriff took the chief's arm and led him through the door which clicked shut after them.

Although the room was empty except for the single deputy, Diff knew that what appeared to be a mirror along the rear wall was a one-way window. The men who had just left the room would now be sitting behind the mirror watching and listening to every word spoken inside.

He had known Deputy Rick Marvel casually for several years. Rick was a large man as Big Red Downs seemed to hire men that were nearly as big as himself. Rick smiled, unlocked the handcuffs, and offered a cigarette.

Diff shook his head to indicate that he didn't smoke.

"Coke, coffee, something like that?" Rick asked politely.

Again a shake of the head as Diff rubbed his wrists where the tight cuffs had irritated the skin.

"Let me tell you something, Diff," Rick said in a calm voice. "They really have it worked out as to how you killed Heather. So if you give us the full details, we can let you cop a guilty plea and that will really make it easier when it comes to sentencing. Like, we could probably get them to go for murder two instead of murder one, maybe even manslaughter if the prosector feels you really cooperated. How does that sound to you? You might get out of the pen in ten years or so if you work with us on this thing."

Diff made a writing gesture in the air.

"Huh?" Rick looked puzzled. "Oh, you can't speak so you want to write with something, is that it?"

Diff nodded.

"Hey, man, I'm real sorry about that. Let me get you something to write with."

The door clicked shut as Rick left the room. The deputy went around a corner to the line of chairs lined up in front of the one-way mirror. Downs, Ray, and the deputies were all sitting in front of the mirror along with a stenographer who was taking notes. A running video recorder mounted on a tripod was pointed at Diff.

"Make sure the recorder is on," Downs said. "And, Rick, you keep at him until he breaks."

"I got a feeling about this guy, Sheriff," the deputy answered. "He's going to be a tough nut to crack."

"That's because he didn't do a damn thing except discover the body for us," Ray said angrily.

"We'll see about that," Downs snapped. "I think he's guilty."

"He needs a pad and pencil," Rick said.

Downs snatched the steno pad from the stenographer, who hurried to get another one. "Hey, the pad is a good thing. The written notes he gives you will be good evidence and will stand up in court better than a voice recording. Make sure you keep everything he writes down."

"Gotcha," Rick said as he returned to the room to hand Diff the pad along with a mechanical pencil he snicked from his breast pocket. "Here you go."

Diff wrote, 'I did not do it.'

"Well, now, I can understand your saying that, but that's not the way it came down, Diff. Now let's look at the whole situation, and you will see why we have it down pretty firm that you are the bad guy in all this." He slapped six large photographs of the Trading Post film scene down on the table. "These were still shots taken by a photographer at the Trading Post the night Heather did her disappearing act. Now in this picture who do we see in the far background?" He pointed to Diff sitting on the lid of his empty trash barrel.

Diff pointed to himself.

"Right we are, Diff, very good. Now we know that Heather disappeared during the few seconds the lights were out even though the square had police guards at all the entrances and exits. They did a very thorough search of the area and guess what? Poof! No Heather. She seemed to just disappear into thin air, right?"

Diff nodded.

"Right you are, my man. Now, we're really getting somewhere. If Heather was not there and we could not find her, where was she?"

Diff shrugged.

"Well, we've worked it out, Diff. It seems pretty apparent to all of us that you knocked her out during the blackout and stuffed her into that empty trash barrel you're sitting on in the picture."

Diff wrote a longer note on his pad. 'I was hired to clean up after the filming and I brought the equipment, including the barrel, down to the square.'

"Sure, I know you did, but then when the lights went out you instantly saw a way to get your hands on Heather. You conked her with something and stuffed her in that barrel."

Diff wrote 'Why?' on his pad.

"I'll get to that later. First, we're talking about how you pulled it off. You waited patiently until things calmed down and the police and bystanders left. When the square was empty, you took her to the graveyard where you planned to do sick things to her. We've worked it out that Heather woke up and wouldn't go along with your game plan and fought back so hard you were forced to shoot her."

Diff shook his head violently.

"We also have firm evidence that places you in the crypt before your fake discovery of the body with Corry."

Diff wrote 'How?" on his pad. 'What evidence do you have?'

Rick reached under the table to pull out a large wrapped object which he placed in front of Diff. He tore the brown wrapping paper off the package to reveal a down sleeping bag. "We found this in the tomb behind the body and we have managed to trace it to you, Diff. That's right, you bought this sleeping bag last winter at the Morgan Camping Outlet. It's a very expensive bag and the sales clerk distinctly remembers selling it to you. Not only do we have an eyewitness to that sale, but there is a written receipt with your name and address on it."

Diff wrote, 'I bought it to give to Corry so he would not freeze to death. My sleeping bag is in the closet at my apartment.'

"Sure. You just happened to give a two-hundred-dollar sleeping bag to the town bum who is so far out of it he doesn't know what day of the week it is."

'Proves nothing,' Diff wrote. 'And you still haven't told me why I supposedly did this.'

"You wanted Heather, didn't you?" Rick said. "You don't date women because of your speech problem, but you are a normal guy who loves beautiful women, isn't that right? You knew she would never go out with you, so when you had the chance you took her. It went bad and you had to kill her. Now, I can understand that, Diff. Maybe a lot of guys would have killed her the way she teased them. Maybe she led you on as sort of a sick joke on her part."

Diff again wrote, 'No!'

Rick raised one eyebrow as far as it would go while he faced the mirror and read the note aloud. "You have written 'No!' You still deny everything even when we have you dead to rights."

Diff wrote another note. 'How did I get her from the square to the cemetery?'

"We wondered about that for a while too," Rick said after he read the note. "But then the sheriff figured it out. You were the one who went down into the sewers, and when you did that, you saw your way out. Later, when everyone left the square, you lowered Heather, still unconscious in the trash barrel, into the sewer. We traced one of those sewer trunk lines, Diff, and one of them leads down to the river and comes out right next to the cemetery. You carried Heather to the cemetery through the sewer."

'I bet there are no tracks,' Diff wrote.

"You lucked out on that one. The rain we had washed away any possible tracks. We've got you dead to rights, Diff. Now do yourself a favor and get it off your chest. Once you give me a full confession you'll feel a lot better."

'No!' Diff wrote in letters that took up a whole page of the pad. He held the note up toward the mirror.

The door burst open as Big Red Downs charged into the room. The massive sheriff had his gun drawn and waved it angrily in the air. "You scum! You rotten killer! You murdered one of the most beautiful women in America! I ought to blow you away right now!"

Other deputies rushed into the room and grabbed Downs and forcibly took away his gun. "Hold on, Sheriff!" Deputy Marvel said. "You don't want to kill this piece of filth. Don't ruin your career over a scumbag.

Let the state execute him for you." They escorted the red-faced sheriff from the room.

"You cooperate with me, Diff, and I'll keep you out of Big Red's hands," Rick said. "Now, if the sheriff has his way, he'd beat a confession out of you."

Diff's note was the longest one he had written since the sheriff's department had brought him in. 'You guys are playing good cop-bad cop with me. Knock it off because I didn't kill her.'

A normal-appearing Sheriff Downs returned to the room followed by Ray and other deputies. His gun was holstered, his flushed face had returned to normal, and his manner seemed placid and businesslike. "Let me see his latest," he said calmly to Rick as he took the last note and read it.

"You know when Diff found Corry with the body, he reported it to me immediately," Ray said.

"Of course he did," Downs replied. "Corry found the body with Diff when he opened the tomb door and so the jig was up. Our killer here had to pretend he had just found Heather's body."

"No!" Holly shouted from the back of the room. "I was with Diff on the day he gave that sleeping bag to Corry. I remember it very well because it was such a grand thing for him to do. He spent his hard-earned money on a homeless man who wouldn't even remember it."

The sheriff's mouth dropped open.

"You can count on what you just heard," Ray said. "My daughter never lies."

"After the model disappeared from the square," Holly continued, "Diff took me home. He was not down in any sewer carrying an unconscious woman to a tomb. I am his alibi and will swear to these things in a court of law."

*   *   *

Holly drove Diff from the sheriff's office back up Main Street toward their house at the top of the hill.

Diff handed her a note. 'Thanks,' it said, 'but I don't remember your being there when I gave the sleeping bag to Corry.'

Holly smiled. "And you didn't take me home the night Heather disappeared either. So I guess Daddy was wrong. I do tell a little fib or two now and then, but it was for a good cause. I know you gave that sleeping bag to Corry and I know you didn't kill Heather. I know those two things with all my heart and soul, Diff, so they weren't much of a lie."

Diff knew that he had nothing to do with Heather's disappearance or death, but Sheriff Downs certainly didn't. The usually angry sheriff was even madder when he had to let Diff go.

It seemed like a good idea to find out how the model disappeared and who killed her. Otherwise, the sheriff and his deputies would be hounding him the rest of his life.

CHAPTER 5

The computer screen winked that new e-mail had arrived as Diff vacuumed the rug in the police chief's office. He had started early that morning so was ahead in his work schedule. He sat at the desk in front of the computer and opened the e-mail account.

As he expected, the newest message was from Holly. He couldn't resist the chance to read it since Ray was in an all-day conference with Sheriff Downs. He used the mouse to click on the message.

'Dear Pops: I have been feeling guilty about something I did yesterday and need to talk with you about it,' the message read.

Diff glanced down at his watch. It was ten in the morning which meant Holly had a free period at the school for the deaf. She was probably in her small office near her computer at this very moment. He typed a brief return message that read, 'Your dad's away for the day so I took a peek at the e-mail. I agree that we have to tell him about the lie. I suspect you are referring to the alibi you gave me yesterday, so I agree we should come clean with Ray.' He typed his name at the end of the message and sent it.

He hoped she would reply and wondered what the response would be. Even if meant that he sat in jail, he could not in all good conscience allow the lie to her father to stand.

A return message blinked on the screen. 'Hi, Diff. Glad you read my note to Pop so now you know how I feel the morning after.'

'Ray is my best friend,' Diff wrote back. 'We have to tell him.'

"Tell me what?" the man who clamped a large hand on Diff's shoulder asked. "And after you tell me what that is, kindly inform me as to why you are reading my personal mail?"

As an answer Diff typed another e-mail message, 'Your father is here and wants to know what we're doing.'

The reply came back nearly in real time. 'Tell him we're trying to get a lie or two off our chests and that we're very sorry,' Holly wrote. 'And tell him that I love him very much.'

Ray reached over Diff's shoulders and typed his own message. 'How about two lies? One, you weren't with Diff when he gave the sleeping bag to Corry, and number two, Diff did not take you home the night of the disappearance. As you may recall, you drove with me that night.'

'Whoops,' was Holly's return message followed by, 'Forgive us, please, and tell Diff that I . . . Never mind.'

'Tell Diff what?' Ray typed back.

'Signing off,' Holly wrote as an ending.

Diff swiveled on the chair to face Ray with a look that transmitted regret to his friend.

"You know," Ray said, "since I took Holly home that night, I am guilty of obstructing justice by not saying so. We have an ethical and legal point here that I can't let sit forever. We have a couple of days until I really have to go to the sheriff on this, Diff. That only gives us a short time to find out how in the hell Heather Mack disappeared and who killed her. We can start by going to the party tonight."

Diff's look transmitted his question.

"The film company is finished here today and they are having what they call a 'wrap party' tonight at the Morgan Lodge. I have an invitation which allows me to bring a companion so I'm taking you as Holly has her own invite. It might be an interesting event since I'm going to ask a couple of people not to leave town until this investigation is over. That's where I need your help and advice, Diff. I'm asking Orson Ordman to stay in Morgan, but I have the feeling there are others in the film crew that I should also require to stay. The question is *who*?"

'Let's find out,' Diff wrote on his pad.

*   *   *

The Morgan Lodge was perched on the crest of Dain Mountain at the far side of the valley. The town of Morgan lay at its feet with Loon Lake and the towering Bald Mountain to the north. The building was a long, rambling affair of log construction with high dormers and a vast front porch that stretched across the front and down one side.

The lodge had been constructed during the turn of the

century by C. Oliver Fisks, a railroad robber baron, who used it as a fall hunting lodge. Its sixty-eight rooms housed his hunting party, gun bearers, and servants. Mr. Fisks, when not busy stealing assets from the railroads he controlled, liked to hunt deer and other helpless animals.

Hard times brought about by new laws and the Depression destroyed Mr. Fisks's financial empire. He met this disastrous group of events by abruptly departing his twentieth-story office without the benefit of an elevator. The lodge had been empty of occupants for more than ten years until the end of the Depression and World War II. In 1945 a returning veteran purchased the lodge for a song and spent two years putting it back together.

The Morgan Lodge now housed guests in all seasons and had a statewide reputation for fine steaks and wine. Another of its major attractions was a two-story combination game-card-dining room with a gigantic stone fireplace at one end that ran parallel to the wide front porch. Those inside the high hall were observed by two dozen antlers from a dozen moose and deer heads, who peered gloomily down from their perches along the balcony.

Ray parked his Morgan police cruiser in the upper parking lot and led Holly and Diff down the path to the lodge's main entrance. As they approached the gaily lit building, they heard music with loud laughter from the gathered models, actors, and technical crew.

The party was well on its way when they went inside the hall. "I can't figure out if this is a memorial party for Heather, a celebration for the end of the filming, or just the way these people eat dinner every night," Ray whispered.

Theater people seem to have a good time, Diff thought.

At one end of the long room, a raised platform held a six-piece orchestra that seemed composed mostly of bongo drums and guitars. At the opposite end of the room, a large movie screen hung from the balcony and stretched nearly to the floor. Long tables filled with bottles of champagne, soft drinks, and appetizers of all sorts were in abundant supply.

"If I wasn't worried about my weight, I'd say let's pig out," Holly said.

Diff didn't need to even glance at her to know that Holly didn't need to worry a second about her weight since it was just about perfect.

"Have fun, kids," Ray said. "I have to talk with our friendly director and his new star. I'm afraid they have to be told to remain in beautiful Morgan a few days longer until our investigation is complete. They are going to love me for that one, and we'll probably see a temper tantrum performance equal to the best of all times."

Ray moved off in search of Orson Ordman and was replaced by the assistant director, the willowy Tracy Zandt, who handed them each a glass of champagne. She raised her glass in a toast, "Here's to it, guys—to our leaving this hick burg and your staying. Down the hatch."

Diff took a large swig and choked while Holly vainly tried to hold back a laugh. *I think he's better in the woods kneeling to drink water from a stream than sipping wine at a party*, she thought.

Orson Ordman was preparing to make a toast. He stood on top of a table at the far end of the room. "Quiet on the set!" he yelled a couple of times until a hush fell over the room. "Tonight we drink to the dead queen." He raised his glass. "To our departed queen, Heather Mack. Long live the new queen, Nell Richards!"

A shocked silence swept through the crowd that

created a strange hush until slight murmurs erupted throughout the room.

As usual, Orson reacted by turning angry. "Ye of little faith, you don't believe me so watch this. Roll the film!" he shouted to the far end of the room as he stepped down from the table and turned to face the screen.

The lights dimmed as the movie screen flickered white. A flash of numbers rolled down the screen before it focused on the scene in front of the Morgan Trading Post. Extras and actors were in the foreground, most of them hooded except for Holly whose flaming red-gold hair accented her beauty.

Nell Richards, wearing a pre-Civil War costume with its wide hoop skirt, stood in the center of the group and walked slowly toward the camera. Her face broke into a wide smile as she approached the camera.

The same scene flipped to another angle as the second camera caught Nell from the side, and then still another view as camera number three filmed her coming down toward the crowd for the third time. The scene had been filmed three times for each take and there had been fifteen takes. The best shots or frames would be selected by the director and film editor after they returned to New York. They would choose from each of the takes from the three different cameras and splice them together in a combination of long, close, and medium shots that seemed to work best for their desired effect.

The camera loved Nell Richards. It caught the fine lines of her cheekbones and the saucy look in her eyes as she merrily walked toward the center camera.

"Is that not our new queen?" Orson yelled from the side.

"Looking good, looking mighty good!" someone else yelled.

"It looks like Mister Director has found himself a new love," Tracy said under her breath only loud enough for Diff and Holly to hear. "If she messes him up like the last one did, maybe she'll do a disappearing act too."

"What are you saying?" Holly asked in a shocked whisper. "You don't mean that."

"Who says I don't?" Tracy said in a hard voice. "I would kill for that man."

"Tracy!" Holly said. "Now is hardly a good time to use that particular group of words. What I mean is, someone was just killed who was fooling with Orson."

Their attention switched back to the screen with its huge pictures of Nell Richards repeating her walk toward the camera. "Everyone agree?" Orson shouted. "Nell is the new queen, right?"

There were more shouts of approval as the lights flicked on again to reveal Nell standing next to Orson at the end of the room. She slowly put her head on his shoulder as he put his arm around her. "Again, to our new star, Nell Richards!" Orson said in toast.

"I wish that was poison," Tracy said as Nell drank.

"If she drops over dead, you are in big trouble," Holly said.

Diff was beginning to wonder if all these people weren't a little bit crazy.

"Hold it right there," Lee Upton said to Diff and Holly. They stood still as the rugged blond man adjusted his still camera lens, took two steps backward as he looked through the viewfinder, and began snapping rapid shots. He took three full-face fronts, went slightly to their side, and took a couple more. "Gotcha," he said as he let the camera dangle from his neck by its band.

"Why us?" Holly asked.

"Not just you, hon," Lee said. "I am shooting the whole shebang on orders of our fearless leader. He wants it all saved for the great film library in the sky."

Hand in hand, Orson Ordman and Nell Richards walked toward them. "Get them on film?" Ordman asked Upton.

"Got their images preserved forever," Lee said.

"Good, because our record wouldn't be complete unless we have the local yokels present and accounted for," Orson said as he dropped Nell's hand and put his arm around Holly. "Did I ever tell you that I love you?" he said with a stage whisper into Holly's ear. "Let's run away together tonight?"

Holly laughed. "Yeah, running away with you would be a crowded event since I think you've asked every woman in this room under seventy."

Orson stepped back in mock horror. "Are you, my darling redhead, accusing me of being unfaithful and fickle?"

"He doesn't have a true-blue bone in his body," Nell said with a laugh. "And don't believe a word he says, especially if he promises you a sports car and jewelry."

Orson held up his hand in mock horror. "And to think I made you a star and you pay me back like this."

Nell took his arm and pulled him away from Holly. "Oh, come on and let's see others in the room." She led him away as Ordman looked back at Holly and winked.

A bell-chime announced dinner. Holly and Diff took seats midway down one of the long tables to find platters of steaks being passed around. Diff saw Ray talking with Orson Ordman at the far corner of the room. As he watched, Orson shook his head violently and Ray responded by shaking his finger at the director. It didn't take much imagination to realize that the chief was telling the director to stay in town for the murder investigation. Ordman did not look happy about it, but he had little choice.

The lodge served simple food: huge New York strip sirloin cooked to order, home fries with onions, and a salad with a rich blue cheese dressing. Holly watched Diff eat a gigantic portion, order a second helping, and still keep shoveling it in. He ate like an elephant and yet he never seemed to gain a pound. Of course, the five miles he ran each morning at dawn might have something to do with keeping the calorie count down.

Things really got rolling after the meal was cleared and the band took up their not necessarily musical but enthusiastic playing. One of the New York actors went out on the porch and did a handstand on the railing, which was fifty feet above a rock cliff. He walked along the balustrade on his hands to the chant of the crowd.

When the dancing began in earnest, Orson Ordman seemed to appear out of nowhere without Nell and took Holly's hand to drag her out on the dance floor. Diff watched the complicated dance for a moment and then walked out on the porch. He saw a couple in the shadows in the far corner holding each other and whispering in voices too low to be heard.

As the clouds blew away from the front of the moon, light fell across the porch to reveal that the kissing couple at the far end were Nell Richards and Lee Upton. When they realized they had been seen, they immediately broke apart as Upton quickly left the porch.

Nell Richards laughed as she walked over to Diff. "You're the man who can't speak, aren't you?"

He nodded.

"Well, speak or not, I think you're cute. The beautiful

thing about not being able to speak is as an actor you wouldn't ever argue over how many lines you had, now, would you?"

The remark was made without ill feeling, but Diff could not help but smile bitterly. He had never considered not speaking as beautiful in any manner.

"Lee and I are old friends," Nell said. "He's a very talented still photographer and that's pretty darn important to a model or actress. A good photo can make you look very beautiful even if you're a plain bunny like me."

For that remark Diff had to write a note. 'You are certainly not plain!' it read.

She laughed again, "You are the only man I know who can't speak but can flirt in a quick note."

"In that case, I just might break his fingers," Holly said as she came out on the porch and took Diff's hand to lead him inside. "It's time you learned to dance before you get in trouble by note writing to pretty models."

Several of the long dining tables had been removed until there was room in front of the stand where the musicians played. The music was loud and the actors and models were enthusiastic as they moved in time to the beat of music.

Diff held back.

Holly pulled on his hand but he refused to move. "Come on now, don't be a stick-in-the-mud. Do it for me because I want to dance."

Diff shook his head violently.

"You've never danced before, have you?" Holly said with a start of realization.

He agreed with that.

"Hey, Red, may I have another dance?" Orson Ordman

said as he took Holly by the waist and without waiting for an answer twirled her off into the crowd of other dancers.

The possibility of dancing terrified Diff. He had never done it, never been taught it, never even seriously considered that he might have to one day. Once in a great while watching television or at the movies he would see dancing in a story, but he couldn't bring himself to do it.

Holly's skirt flared as she twirled and threw her head back with a laugh. The tempo of the music picked up as the pace of the dance increased.

As Diff looked at Orson looking at Holly, he was reminded of a hunting mountain lion viewing a plump deer just prior to the leap that would bring the defenseless deer down.

He'd been through a lot with Holly. They had been shot at, had been nearly killed in a car accident, and had always managed to come through without injury. Tonight could turn into a crisis of a different sort and be very serious business. He couldn't go after her. He couldn't bring himself to do it.

He knew he had to go out on that dance floor although he'd rather go into a dark cave that might be filled with angry bears. It had to be done. He forced himself to feel the music and to imagine a cougar he had once seen on a rock rim on Bald Mountain. The big cat had moved with an unbelievable grace as if walking to the rhythm of the wind. The animal's muscles had rippled under his skin as he moved in that marvelous catlike manner.

He felt the music. He could sense the throb and beat from the drums on the stand.

He could imitate animals because he had nearly grown up in the woods. He had learned from them when they had been the only life he was allowed. He thought of that mountain cat again and felt the animal's graceful movements and rhythm.

He could do it. He could move like that to the throb and beat of the drums.

Diff went out on the dance floor at the moment Holly was flung away from Orson Ordman in a very complicated dance step. He swept her up in his arms as they moved to the music.

For these moments, she was his as they danced with a grace and rhythm that made the others circle around to watch.

Orson picked up the beat with clapping hands which in turn was taken up by others until only Diff and Holly danced while everyone else beat out the rhythm in a clapping cadence.

CHAPTER 6

Diff was mopping the floor in front of the holding cells located toward the rear of police headquarters when Sally Way came through the back door. The pregnant former communications clerk took the mop out of his hands.

"Hi, Daddy," she said.

Diff shook his head in a violent no.

"Well, you know that," Sally said with a crooked smile. "And I know you aren't the father, but no one else in the world knows. Now, my gorgeous hunk, what that means is that you have exactly one week to propose marriage to me or the whole town starts calling you daddy."

Diff shook his head and wrote 'DNA test' on his pad and gave her the note.

She laughed. "I intend to be Mrs. Diff James by the

time you get around to that. Came to pick up my last paycheck," Sally said as she started down the hall after waving good-bye. "Toodle-oo, Daddy-o."

Ray's office door opened and the chief beckoned to Diff. The mop went back in its bucket, the "wet floor" sign propped back near the wall, and Diff went to the office.

When Ray closed the office door, Diff saw the still photographer, Lee Upton, sitting on the leather sofa along the side wall. Lee wore a camera vest filled with extra lenses, packets of film, and other items and gadgets unknown to Diff.

"Lee has asked my permission to do a photo story on you, Diff," Ray said.

Diff sat by the edge of the desk and scrawled a note on his pad which he handed to the chief.

'A story about a janitor is not a very interesting topic. I would guess it would have very limited readership.'

Ray laughed and handed the note to Lee. "Good point," the photographer said with a smile. "I'm not particularly interested in your janitorial abilities as much as I am in your tracking and other special help you provide the police. Of course, we'll probably need to go into your general background. I'm thinking about a couple of good mood shots of that hole where you were held prisoner during most of your childhood and adolescence."

Diff stood up so quickly his straight chair fell backwards with a clatter. He strode out the door into the hall and back to his bucket where he grabbed the mop and slapped it down on the hall floor. He began to make wide sweeping passes along the floor with an exertion that he hoped would dull his anger.

Lee Upton hurried down the hall. "Hey, I'm sorry," he said. "No kidding, Diff, I didn't realize that I was revealing a confidence and that you were so sensitive about your background. I just didn't know, okay?" He held out his hand.

Diff paused in his frenzied mopping and looked at the photographer who was smiling at him in a friendly manner. He realized it wasn't this man's fault. The story of his background was not a secret. There were dozens of people in town who knew his history. In fact, there weren't many secrets in a small city like Morgan.

Diff dipped his mop back in its bucket and grasped Lee's hand.

"When I heard they were going to use you again to do some tracking, I realized that it would be a good opportunity to do a photo story. I'm stuck in this town for a while anyway, so why not put my time to good use?"

The chief came out of his office and walked toward them as Diff looked at Ray with unspoken questions.

It was Ray's turn to smile. "You stormed out of my office too fast for me to tell you. We have to bring in a temp worker to do the floors again as we need you to track down an escapee."

'Who?' Diff wrote in the note he gave to Ray.

"Haven't you heard? Corry walked away from the psych ward early this morning. The guy got out of a closed ward by getting into a locked linen room where he hid under a laundry cart. He rode out of the ward hidden under the linen cart. They can't figure out how he did it, so my first assignment is for you and Holly to go to the hospital and find out how he escaped. The second assignment is to find him."

"And I have permission to go along and take pictures," Lee Upton said.

Diff shook his head.

The photographer put his hand on Diff's shoulder. "You know, the magazine article that comes out of this could change your life."

"It won't do any harm," Holly said as she came down the hall.

"When I got word Corry was gone, I did something I should have done before," Ray said.

The police chief knew that the hunch of Diff's shoulders meant, *Did what?*

"To answer your question, I searched Corry's cart after I got word he had escaped. After Toms took him to the hospital, we brought his cart with all his possessions here to the station. We stuck it down in the boiler room out of the way. It never occurred to me to look through his stuff as I never seriously considered Corry a suspect. I changed my mind when he pulled his disappearing act from the hospital. That little caper proved that he wasn't as far out in left field as we all thought. Come on, I'll show you what I found."

In single file they went down the corridor to the cellar steps at the far end of the hall. Their shoes clanked on the metal stairwell as they went into the basement which held the locker room, indoor pistol range, and the boiler room at the far end of the building.

Corry's cart was on its side in the far corner opposite the boiler. Its contents were spread out in neat rows along the cement floor.

The first item Ray picked up was a large brown paper bag which he turned upside down. Dozens of magazine photographs fluttered to the bare concrete. Lee and Diff picked up several of the pictures.

Each picture was of a very alive Heather Mack at the height of her modeling career. The Vietnam veteran must have spent a great deal of his pension money on magazines as he seemed to have collected every advertisement the model ever posed for. He was particularly fond of one ad for a trendy bikini bathing suit as he had half a dozen copies. Included in the collection were news and magazine articles about Heather, such as a recent one titled, "Supermodel to Have Movie Career."

"It would seem that the homeless population of the city of Morgan was pretty well smitten by Heather Mack," Ray said.

"The guy was obviously bonkers over her," Lee said.

"So we now have a very interesting situation," Ray said. "Corry is found in a crypt with the dead model. We now know that he was quite an admirer of that beautiful woman who disappeared until he just *happened* to find her. Another fact we have is that before I discover these connections, Corry takes off. All of this leads me to believe that he may be our killer."

"I've taken hundreds of shots of Heather," Lee said. He gestured to the mass of pictures on the floor. "I took a bunch of those for various magazines, but that doesn't mean I was bonkers over the woman. There must be thousands of men in this country who thought Heather was the most beautiful woman in the world."

"There was a pistol wrapped in a dirty towel in this stuff," Ray said. "I sent it over to the state police lab, and ballistics has established it as the murder weapon. We have our killer all right."

"Correction, you don't have your killer," Lee said.

"We'll get him," Ray answered.

"If you can find him," Lee added.

"Diff will find him," Ray said.

*   *   *

Holly drove them to the Idle Hours Motel so that Lee Upton could pick up some camera equipment. Diff sat next to her and read the file on Corry that Ray had given them as they left the police station.

He discovered for the first time that Corry's last name was Dade and that he was a decorated Vietnam veteran. The medal citation stated that he had received the Bronze Star for heroic service as a "cave rat."

"Cave rats," or "hole moles" as they were sometimes known in Vietnam, were the men who went into underground bunkers after the enemy. After a tunnel system was discovered, explosives were dropped in the hole. It was necessary after that for someone to go down through the opening and explore what was inside. The brave men who did this were usually thin men who could wiggle and squirm through the narrow tunnels. They carried a flashlight and only a pistol for protection when they went into these very dangerous places. It was their job to report to the surface the number of enemy inside the network and also to locate any useful information such as maps.

It was very dangerous work and most men were only able to do it for a few weeks at a time before they were given another assignment. Corry had done it for seven months before he cracked. Early one morning he had gone into a very deep cave and not come out. The next day another "cave rat" had gone inside to look for him. He found Corry in a deep hospital bunker surrounded by dead men. He was sitting on the dirt floor staring into the dark with a burned-out flashlight in one hand

and an empty pistol in the other.

Corry had been given a medal and discharged for medical reasons. The fear that grew in him during those many hours in the tunnels had never disappeared.

He had returned to his home in Morgan only to find that his mother and father had been killed in a car wreck the day before his arrival. He had allowed the house to be foreclosed as he could not bring himself to sleep there or anywhere else for more than one night at a time. Now he walked the streets of Morgan looking for that night's place to sleep, and the townspeople paid little attention to the homeless man they hardly saw.

Diff slowly shut the file. Now he knew why he felt such a kinship to the homeless man. They had both suffered in holes under the ground and had found in those places the depths of terror that can live in a man's soul.

He did not think that Corry had killed Heather Mack. He did not think the former veteran was capable of killing anyone or anything now or in the future. The combat veteran had already been through a killing hell.

Diff knew that it was up to him to find the homeless man before some cop did—because he knew that Corry would run from the police and might be shot and killed.

They arrived at the Idle Hours Motel and parked in front of Lee's unit.

"How come you're staying on in Morgan?" Holly asked. "You aren't one of the crew my father asked to stay on."

"Nell and I have been going around together, and so I'm staying to give her moral support," Lee said. "If I have my way, she's going to be the next Heather Mack. She's got the features for it and photographs beautifully."

They followed Lee up the walk to his unit and went inside after he unlocked the door. The room's walls were covered with photographs of the commercial the film crew had been shooting in Morgan.

Holly looked at some of the pictures to see that many which included Nell also had her in the background. "Hey, wow!" she said.

"Like them?" Lee asked with a smile. "I developed most of them yesterday when, as a matter of professional courtesy, the Morgan newspaper let me use their darkroom. I'll need a long-distance lens for this excursion," Lee said as he rummaged through a camera bag looking for what he needed. "I want to capture it all on film when you find this guy. Where do we go first?"

Holly glanced over at Diff, who was looking carefully at the photographs tacked on the walls. "What do you think, Diff? Where do we go first?"

Diff was intrigued with the pictures and did not take the time to write a note to Holly, but signed a message to her.

Holly read his moving hand signals. "We're going to the hospital and find out exactly how Corry got out of a locked ward," she translated.

"Good point," Lee said. "A guy who can make himself disappear out of a locked ward may be just the person to make an actress disappear from a movie set in front of a hundred people."

"Interesting about his military career," Holly said as she flipped through the file Diff had been reading on the trip to the motel. "I read here that Corry was a 'cave rat' in Vietnam."

"No kidding?" Lee asked. "A man that could do that sort of dangerous stuff might very easily have been able to get into the sewers with Heather."

"Diff didn't think so since he didn't see any footprints down there," Holly said.

The Morgan Hospital was a four-story building located at the far end of Main Street. They were met at the front desk by Kelly, the security guard, who had been alerted by Ray that they were on their way. He took them to the locked ward on the fourth floor where he pressed a buzzer on the heavy metal door leading into the unit.

"Never had one of them escape before," Kelly said. "Usually they're on such heavy medication that they aren't in condition to go anywhere."

The door was opened by a male nurse dressed in immaculate white pants and T-shirt. His massive arms bulged in the short-sleeved shirt. He nodded at Kelly and spoke in a high voice that seemed odd coming from such a large man.

"Mr. Corry decided he did not like sleeping in the same place two nights in a row," he said. "He told me he was going to have to leave, and by golly, he did."

"He told you that in advance?" Holly asked.

"Sure did. On the afternoon of his second day he said he'd have to go now and find another place to sleep. Of course, we all laughed at that one, but boy, how wrong can you get?"

"How did he get out?" Kelly asked.

"I'll show you," the male nurse said as he took a large key ring from his belt and selected a small key. He went to another metal door only a few feet from the entrance which had a narrow metal chute cut into its face. "We drop dirty linen and towels through this small opening," the nurse said as he unlocked the door and swung it open. Inside the narrow room was a large canvas laundry cart on wheels. "You can see how the linen falls through the chute opening into the cart. Once a day an orderly takes the cart out of the locked closet and wheels it through another locked door out to the elevator. It's taken down to the basement and left outside the laundry room. Patient Corry somehow got into this room through a locked door, climbed into the cart, and covered himself with dirty sheets. He wasn't seen by the orderly and was wheeled out of the ward to the basement. Down there one of the laundry workers saw him climb from the cart and run out to the street."

"Then the problem is, how did he get into the linen closet?" Kelly asked for everyone.

"You got it," the nurse said. "I've got the only set of keys to this room. When I go off duty, I turn them over to the other head nurse when she comes in. Corry never had them because they never leave the body of the charge nurse."

Diff stepped inside the small room to feel along the walls. He pounded in several places without hearing an echo which indicated to him that the walls were solid. He carefully examined the floor and ceiling before settling on the ceiling where he pointed to a metal grid.

"That's only an air vent," the nurse said. All the rooms have them for heat and central air conditioning.

Diff balanced on the rim of the laundry cart and pushed open the grate that covered the vent.

"The vents are all connected," the nurse said, "but nothing except a rat could get through that space."

Diff climbed down and wrote on his pad, 'One did.'

"No way," the nurse said. "The only kinda guy who could do that would be like I saw when I was a medic in Nam. Maybe one of those tunnel rats that went down . . .”

Diff nodded as the nurse slapped his own forehead.

Diff wrote another note. ‘I know where Corry is, so we had better go get him.’

*   *   *

Lee Upton took three shots of the entrance to the Morgan Cemetery before they pulled open the rusting front gate and went inside. They walked in single file along the stone path toward the crypts in the center of the plots.

“Hey, I get it,” Lee said as he took a moving shot of Diff in the lead. “You think our crazy veteran returned to the scene of the crime?”

Without breaking stride, Diff signed his answer to Holly.

“Diff says no,” Holly repeated to Lee. “He says Corry would come back here for his stuff.”

“That cart of belongings containing all his junk is in the police headquarters basement,” Lee said.

“We know that, but Corry doesn’t,” Holly answered. “He probably still remembers he left his cart parked next to where the body of Heather was found. This is where he’d come after his escape.”

“Hey, that does make sense,” Lee said as he slammed a roll of fresh film into his camera. “This I got to get all down on film. If he’s here, Diff is going to be the hero cop of the hour.”

“Diff is not a cop,” Holly said sadly. “He would like to be, but because of his . . . well, he just can’t.”

They came to the tomb where Heather’s body was discovered and pushed the rusting door open to find the inside empty except for the stone crypt.

"Well, so much for that," Lee said as he snapped a closeup of Diff and Holly's disappointed faces. "Our homeless man is not as far out to lunch as you think. He knows enough to be over the state line by now, maybe even over the border into Canada."

Diff noticed that the stone slab covering the crypt was pushed slightly open. He pushed it further to reveal Corry sleeping on his side on top of a sealed coffin.

"I'll be," Lee said, too dumbfounded to snap a picture with the camera he held in his hands.

CHAPTER
7

They stood in a semicircle at the police station parking lot as the private bus belonging to Heather Mack was towed in. "Any of you have keys to this thing?" Ray asked.

"I don't see why we have to do this," Orson Ordman snapped. "The woman is dead and you've slapped the killer in jail. Why don't you leave her private things alone?"

Diff stood behind and slightly to the right of Ray, with Holly on his left, while the movie company people stood in a half circle in front of them. As usual the director, Orson Ordman, had the center position with Nell Richards on his right and Lee Upton on the left. Tracy Zandt, the ever faithful assistant, stood a discreet three steps behind Orson.

"We have a suspicious-acting homeless man in custody," Ray answered. "However, our investigation is still ongoing as we consider all possibilities."

"I understand he was obsessed with Heather, you found him in the graveyard with her body, and he had the murder weapon. What more do you want besides an eyewitness?" Ordman continued impatiently. "Or a confession which he is probably too out of it to give?"

"A full confession would help, and why don't you shut up?" Ray answered in kind.

"I don't have to take this," Orson said as he turned and strode toward his Jaguar parked in front of the building.

Ray looked after the emotional director a moment before he pointed a finger at Ordman's back and beckoned. Sergeant Ned Toms immediately accepted the command and ran after Ordman to put a restraining hand on the man's shoulder.

Orson shrugged the hand away and mumbled, "Leave me alone!"

Ned twirled the director around, bent him forward, and snapped handcuffs on his wrists. He led him back to the circle in front of Ray.

"I'll have your hide for this!" Orson yelled. "You'll never work again in this state, and you'll be on welfare before I'm through with you!"

"Oh, Orson, shut up," Tracy said with a sigh.

"You're fired!" Orson snapped at her.

"You've already fired me twice yesterday and once earlier this morning," Tracy said. "Who else would put up with you?"

"Knock it off, you two," Ray said in a quiet but authoritative voice. He nodded toward Sergeant Toms who immediately unlocked the handcuffs. Orson took the obvious hint and didn't move.

"Now listen up," Ray commanded. "As most of you know, we have discovered the murder weapon in the possession of the homeless man."

"Then why can't we leave and go back to New York City?" Nell Richards asked.

"Because we traced the murder weapon and found that the gun was legally registered to Heather Mack," Ray said.

There was stunned silence.

"How could that be?" Holly finally asked. "How on earth could Corry get his hands on it?"

"He stole it, of course," Orson muttered under his breath.

"It could be because it is," her father answered. "Heather bought the gun in Virginia, had it legally registered in New York, and had a permit for it. We asked the New York Police Department to search her apartment."

"And . . . ?" Orson Ordman asked.

"And nothing," Ray shot back. "The gun permit was found but nothing else of importance. The question is, was there ammunition, a holster, anything else that might have been part of the package? We also want to check for any sign of forced entry into the bus, the theft of other items, and any other clues that might be here. That's why we're going into her private bus by forcing the door."

Sergeant Toms stepped forward to insert a crowbar into the door seam.

"Wait a minute, I can answer questions as to why she had the gun," Orson said. "After all, I was married to her for four years. I know she carried the gun in the bus whenever she went on location." He reached into his pocket and pulled out a key ring. "There's no need to break down the door since I have a key."

"Do you, now?" Ray said. "That's interesting."

Orson gave Ray a dirty look as he stepped to the side of the bus and inserted his key into the door lock. A camera flash flared as Lee Upton snapped a picture of the bus door opening.

Ray pushed Orson away from the open door. "You stay out here," he said as he went inside followed by Ned Toms and Diff.

The outside of the bus looked like an ordinary long-distance carrier except that there were fewer side windows. A few feet back from the driver there was one long window on each side and that was made of heavily tinted glass so that no one could see inside.

The driver's compartment had four seats for passengers but was separated from the living quarters by another door that led to Heather's personal compartment.

Ray pushed open the second door and they went inside. The interior was like a small apartment with a sitting area that had two couches facing each other separated by a coffee table. A large TV with VCR and stereo record player was built into the wall next to a dry sink and bar. In the center of the bus was a small kitchen with a built-in table and chairs. The third and final door led into Heather's bedroom and private bath with shower.

"A nice way to travel," Ray said. "Well, let's get to it," he said as they began to make a careful search of the doors and closets inside the compartment.

Ray and Ned Toms searched inside while Diff checked underneath the bus and inside the luggage compartment and even climbed on the roof. The search took the better part of an hour of hard work.

When they were finished, the three men sat in the dining alcove of the bus. "I think this is important," Ray said as he placed a gun holster and box of ammunition on the table in front of them. "The ammunition is the right caliber and the holster would fit the weapon, so I think that establishes that in all probability she had the pistol with her."

Diff wrote a note. 'I can't believe that Corry broke into the bus to take that gun. It's not like him since he usually stays away from people and has never been known to steal.'

Both police officers nodded in agreement.

"I think it's interesting that her jewelry was all here. Whoever took the gun did not have any interest in some very valuable diamonds," Sergeant Toms said.

"Get the others in here," Ray said.

Toms went outside and brought Lee Upton, Nell Richards, and Tracy Zandt inside the bus.

Ray displayed the gun holster and box of ammunition to them. "Any of you know about these things?"

"Sure," Tracy said. "Like Orson said, she always carried that gun with her. She was raised in Texas and felt that she knew how to handle guns so that no bad guy was going to get at her."

"Then you knew it was kept in here?" Ray asked.

"Sure," Tracy answered. "I knew it."

"So did I," Lee and Nell answered simultaneously.

"How come?" Ray said.

Nell spoke, "Heather had a lot of publicity which made her somewhat famous. She'd get all kinds of letters and crazy phone calls. Fans would sit outside her apartment building for days just to catch a glimpse of her. She was stalked and wooed by lots of weirdos. You know, it could be a stalker who did this to her. Those guys can be really nuts and seem to never give up."

"Maybe," Ray said. "Now let me get this straight. You

all knew the gun was here?" They all nodded. "And Orson knew it also." They nodded again. "Who had access to the bus?" Ray asked.

Tracy pulled a key from her pocket and held it up. "As Orson's assistant I had keys to everything he did."

"We both had keys too," Nell Richards said as she put her hand on Lee's shoulder. "I sometimes helped Heather with her makeup, so I needed access, and Lee used to store some of his valuable cameras in here when we were on the road."

"And where is Orson?" Ray asked.

"You got me," Lee Upton said as he rapidly snapped pictures of the bus interior.

Diff also wondered where Holly was.

*   *   *

When Diff turned his pickup into the driveway leading to the garage, he noticed the parked Jaguar containing a couple sitting extremely close together. He cut his engine and came to a silent halt by the rear bumper of the expensive sports car.

The man and woman in front of him were not aware that he was there. He wondered if they were aware of anything or anyone else in the world since they were locked in a close embrace.

Diff was stunned.

He could not believe what he was seeing not ten feet away. Although he did not see her face because the man's head blocked his view, the bright golden-red hair told him who was in the car more clearly than if she carried a huge sign.

Holly saw him. "I've got things to do," she said loud enough for him to hear as she jumped from the car.

Orson Ordman leaped out of the car after her as she dashed for the rear door. "Hey, come on, Red, I didn't mean any harm." He caught up to her before she went inside and pulled her back. "Now come on, baby, let's talk this over. You were giving me the come-on."

Diff slammed from his pickup and walked across the yard toward the arguing couple. His mind whirled in confusion and hurt, but he would not let this man bully Holly no matter what they had been doing in the Jaguar.

Orson saw Diff and immediately dropped Holly's arm, allowing her to dash away to her front door.

"Now wait a minute, guy," Orson said. "I haven't any quarrel with you, okay? No harm done, right?" Orson held up his palms in a gesture of peace. "So let's calm down and take it easy. I didn't mean any harm to your girl. I read her signal that she wanted me to kiss her and she wasn't exactly fighting me off."

Diff was about to take a swing at the movie director's face when Holly cried out, "No, Diff, don't! He's right. I did lead him on."

Diff dropped his hand and wheeled to run up the steps to his apartment. He threw himself on the couch to stare at the ceiling a moment before he catapulted to his feet to go to the window.

Holly was standing by the screen door talking in a low voice to Orson Ordman. Orson shook his head before he leaned over and kissed her forehead. He gave Holly a jaunty wave and drove the car around Diff's truck and down the drive. He turned up the street with a squeal of tires and a roar of the Jag's powerful engine.

Holly stood looking after the director a moment before she glanced up at Diff's apartment. Their eyes met across the distance.

Diff was the first to turn away because he could not bear her sympathy.

*   *   *

Holly watched him turn away from his window and disappear into the interior of the room. She wanted to run up the steps and pound on the door until he opened it and she threw herself into his arms.

She knew he would reject her. She knew he watched over her like a big brother would after a younger sister. He was suspicious of the movie director, and he was probably right. Orson was doing everything in his power to get her to return to New York City with the rest of the film crew. He kept telling her how her hair made her different from most other actresses and models.

When she and Orson were in the Jaguar, she had turned her head away from him until she saw Diff pull up behind them in his pickup. It was in that one moment that she made a very bad mistake. For a brief instant she wanted to make Diff jealous, and she had kissed Orson before she jumped from the car.

She was horrified when she saw Diff's look of utter dismay. She fought the urge to run to his pickup and tell him that it wasn't what he thought—she wasn't really interested in Orson. She was interested in Diff James, and why wouldn't he stop treating her like a sister and look at her as a woman?

*   *   *

Diff thought it only natural that Holly loved Orson Ordman. The director did have his faults, such as his uncontrollable temper, and he certainly liked to have his own way in all matters. However, he was almost famous, he probably had money, and he could certainly talk well. It was no wonder that Holly found him to be an attractive man and a far better catch than a mute janitor with no future beyond mopping floors for the next thirty years.

Orson probably saw in Holly what Diff did. The director was intelligent enough to realize that she was kind and generous with a great sense of humor. She had such a feeling for life that it made anyone with her have strong emotions toward the most ordinary things. She was attractive. No, Diff thought, she was beautiful.

He could not speak so he could not tell her how he felt; and because he could not speak, he had nothing to offer her. And yet, he couldn't stand to see her in the arms of anyone else. He would have to leave Morgan. He would travel to a place far away from the woman he loved.

Diff walked slowly through his small apartment to the bedroom where he began to pack.

CHAPTER
8

Diff James did not own a suitcase so he packed underwear and socks in his backpack and threw extra pants and shirts in a cardboard carton before he boxed his computer and its components. There was a good deal of outdoor items, fishing gear, and camping equipment that he would need for a life on the road.

He stood before his overflowing bookcase and was sad to realize that there was no way for him to take all of his beloved books with him. He would only be able to take the ones that were the most important to him. He ran his hands lightly over their spines with the realization of how much pleasure they had given him since Holly had taught him to read.

He picked up a copy of Jack London's *Call of the Wild*. It was one of the first adult books he had read. It would always have a special place for him because of the author's feeling for the outdoors and animals. He pulled out that one to take with him along with half a dozen others that were his special favorites.

When he reverently packed his favorite fly rod, he remembered that Ray had often admired it. He owed the man more than he could ever repay and decided to leave the fishing rod and its case in a prominent place so that Ray would discover it and realize it was Diff's final gift. The sleeping bag and grasshopper propane stove were the last items stowed in the truck bed.

He waited until the last light in the big house winked out before he covered the boxes with a plastic sheet which he securely tied down.

He slid behind the wheel, shoved the drive into neutral, and released the brake. The pickup crept down the driveway's slight incline into the street. He used the vehicle's forward momentum to turn and coast down the hill. When he reached the end of the block, far enough from the house so that his engine ignition would not be heard, he started the truck.

While the engine idled, he turned for a final look at the place he had called home for so long. The two people he loved the most in this world lived there. The older man was his boss, teacher, and close friend who would be greatly missed. The woman he loved with a passion he could not voice also lived there, and he wondered if she could ever be replaced in his life.

The people he was leaving had led him into a new life that was now over. His own deep feelings had forced him into a position where for everyone's benefit he must leave. He could not risk betraying Ray's trust or allow himself to even dream of taking advantage of Holly's sisterly feelings.

Seeing her every day, spending hours by her side, and

knowing she slept only a few feet away was more than he could stand. Since he could not speak, he felt incapable of expressing his feeling for her in any other way.

His attraction to Holly meant that he could not stay in Morgan another day.

He threw the truck in gear and sped down Main Street toward the far end of town. He didn't have firm plans, but perhaps he would travel across the country and see America. He would sleep in the open when he was tired, and during the day he would cruise secondary highways and out-of-the-way places as his feelings directed.

He had money saved in the bank since his rent was cheap, he ate half his meals with Ray and Holly, and he spent most of his free time in the woods or fishing distant streams. Often he would not even cash his monthly paycheck and would have to be reminded by the City Treasurer to deposit it. He patted the wallet in his right pants pocket, knowing that inside its flap was his ATM card. That little piece of plastic was a marvel of modern life that meant he could stop at a bank machine anywhere in the country and draw cash.

He accelerated past the Morgan Bar and Grill on the outskirts of town and turned down Route 40, which was a straight path toward the distant New York State Thruway. By dawn he would be three hundred miles away in a place where he would be unknown.

He was ten miles out of Morgan when a police cruiser driving behind him blinked on its bubblegum roof lights. Its siren whined briefly and abruptly died as Diff pulled to a stop on the shoulder.

He watched in the rearview mirror as the sheriff's department car braked to a halt behind him. A uniformed deputy slowly left the cruiser and lightly brushed his hand along the butt of the gun at his hip as he walked toward the pickup.

"Where in the hell are you going at this time of night, Diff?" Deputy Marvel asked.

Diff looked at the man without an answer.

The deputy stiffened angrily, "I asked you a question, mister, and I want an . . ." In the beam of the patrol car's headlights the deputy flushed with embarrassment. "Hey, man, I'm sorry. I keep forgetting you can't speak. I know you can write it out for me. So tell me why you're moving like a bat out of hell and where in the hell you're going at this time of night."

Diff wrote a quick note that he handed through the window. 'Just out for a drive on this fine evening.'

The deputy read the note. "Uh-huh. Just out for a drive. Well, let me tell you something. The sheriff didn't much buy into your murder alibi, Diff. He's had us keeping an eye on you since the day you walked out of his office. If I were you, I wouldn't try and go anywhere until this case is closed. Do you read me?"

Diff nodded.

"Okay, now here's the way it goes. If you turn around and go back home, nothing happens. If you try and continue toward the Thruway, I'm hitting you with a dozen moving violations so serious I'll have to take you in. Got that lay of the land, Old Buddy?"

Diff nodded yes.

"Then we're turning back, aren't we?"

Diff knew he had no choice. He made a U-turn and drove slowly back toward the house on the hill that held the woman he loved.

As he approached the city limits, he passed the Morgan Bar and Grill, which was the last building at the town line. Two flashing neon beer signs in the bar's front window gave a final blink as they were switched off. Diff glanced at the dashboard clock to see that it was bar closing time and they were locking the place up.

The Laman brothers' pickup was the last vehicle parked in front of the bar. Diff had a vivid memory of the attacking rats in the sewer under the square. Once again he felt them run over his body when the rope that held him was dropped and he fell into the muck where the rats could begin to bite and nip.

Everyone in town knew that the Laman brothers had volunteered to help lower him into that sewer. Perhaps only he knew that they had deliberately dropped the rope. Tonight of all nights, the remembered anger and the long-standing feud with the brothers broke through his emotional control and filled him with rage.

Diff lost it.

He slammed on the brakes, which threw the truck into a skid that plunged it into the side of the brothers' pickup. There was a wrench of screeching metal as his plow plate attachment tore off the Lamans' front fender. Diff backed and then sped forward again to slam into the side of the pickup for the second time.

"What the hell!" Luke Laman yelled from the doorway of the bar.

"That guys is nuts!" his brother added.

Diff backed again and rammed his truck forward with enough force to push the other truck sideways until it smashed against the building. The plow attachment on his front grill tangled with the torn metal of the brothers' truck, and he ground to a halt. He threw the gear in reverse, but the death grip of the mortally wounded Laman truck would not release him.

His side door jerked open as hands reached in to pull him into the drive. Heavy boots kicked at his head and belly as he rolled over and fought to regain his feet.

"Let me at the fink!" Luke yelled as he charged at Diff.

The Morgan Bar's bartender, Four Eyes Marlee, stood in the doorway with a cellular phone in one hand and a baseball bat in the other. He screamed over the phone at the 911 operator.

"There's murder out here! They are going to kill each other!" he shouted.

Diff parried Luke's blow with his shoulder and shot out a fist as Joe Laman climbed on his back, which knocked all three men down in a grunting heap. Four Eyes dropped the phone and grabbed his baseball bat with both hands as he ran toward them.

A police siren sounded in the distance as it sped to the scene.

*   *   *

When he awoke, Diff knew he was in a Morgan holding cell because he recognized the pattern of web cracks on the floor he had mopped hundreds of times. His head hurt and he gingerly felt the lump already swelling at the side of his head. Four Eyes must have really connected with that baseball bat. He hoped the Laman brothers received a little of the same punishment.

Sergeant Ned Toms walked slowly down the hall smoking his ever-present pipe and carrying a clipboard with a partially completed report. When Diff sat up, waves of pain circled in his eyes with wrenching black rings. Four Eyes, the Laman brothers, or both had really done a number on him. He hurt so much he was afraid he was going to die, and then as the pain continued, he was afraid he might live.

Ned stopped in the hallway in front of the cell and leaned against the wall with the clipboard tucked under his arm. He puffed smoke rings while he looked at Diff and slowly shook his head. "You really lost it out there, didn't you?"

Diff nodded and that made his head hurt even more.

"It might interest you to know that by the time we got to the Morgan Bar, all three of you were unconscious. Four Eyes can swing a mean baseball bat."

Diff jerked his finger toward the wall indicating that he assumed the brothers were in the cell next door.

"Only other person in that cell is old Corry. No way did I want you and the Lamans together in the same building," Toms said. "The brothers gruesome are residing in two of the sheriff's holding cells. We're charging all three of you with breach of peace, disturbing the peace, assault, and here we list you on them and them on you, mischievous mischief, and a few other crimes we're still working on. For that bag of miscellaneous charges you'll probably get off with a fine and a bunch of community service, but it looks like you blew your job, Diff. You know there's no way Ray Wilson can keep you on after all this comes out in open court. If what the Laman brothers say is true, that you deliberately destroyed their truck, it could mean time for you."

Diff nodded and shrugged. The way this day was going that might be another way to get away from Holly besides running away to see America. With this option, he was going to see even less of the country than he had anticipated.

Ned clenched the pipe between his teeth as he began to write on the form attached to the clipboard. "Now, I've got to finish my report on this incident. We have it down the way Four Eyes saw the fight. He says you three were really going at it. Like I told you, it's assault charges and breach of peace on all of you. Now, what I don't have is that business about the moving vehicle accident."

Diff shrugged.

"Now, the way I see it," Ned Toms said, "is that you were driving along the road obeying the speed limit when you lost vehicle control and accidentally smashed into the Laman brothers' pickup. Perhaps there was a mechanical failure in your truck. Or maybe you just fell asleep and accidentally rammed into their truck. Now, we know the Laman brothers were leaving the bar when all this happened. Since they are not rocket scientists and are quick to anger, when they saw how you damaged their vehicle, the fight started. So we can settle the fight business by saying that they attacked you and you were forced to defend yourself. Now, is that telling an accurate recounting of what happened?"

Diff shrugged.

"Good!" Ned Toms smiled as he made notes on his report. "We seem to be getting somewhere. Now, we know that they attacked an innocent bystander after an unfortunate accident. You know, the way this is going to come out, we might save your job after all. I see you as a perfectly innocent, hard-working janitor with a speech handicap who runs off the road and accidentally damages the town bums' truck. Since our innocent janitor cannot speak, he is unable to inform said bums that it was all a mistake and his insurance company will pay all damages. The twins do not understand what happened and proceed to attack said solid citizen. When Mr. Solid defends himself, he is accidentally felled by a baseball bat swung by a half-blind bartender. Hey, this is looking better and better all the time. You're going to come out whole on this thing, Diff."

Diff signaled that he wanted the clipboard. Ned Toms looked at him with a raised eyebrow and then slowly handed it through the bars.

"I'd be careful what I wrote on that report, Diff," Ned said. "If it came down like I said . . . you skidded off the road for one reason or another and accidentally rammed into their truck . . . and then they attacked you . . . you come out whole in this whole damn mess. If it comes down another way, you might have a mite of difficulty."

Diff wrote in the space provided on the report form, 'I deliberately stopped at the Morgan Bar when I recognized the brothers' pickup. I was very angry with them, and I rammed into the side of their vehicle not once but several times until I felt that I had demolished it. I would have driven away but the two vehicles were stuck together in a mess of twisted metal. I was pulled from my truck by the brothers. The fight started when I took a swing at Luke or maybe it was Joe.' He finished the remarks with a flourish, inserted two exclamation points, and signed his name in very large letters.

Diff handed the clipboard with the finished report back to Ned Toms, who took a few moments to carefully read it. "This will hang you, Diff." Their eyes met through the bars. "But it's the truth, isn't it?"

Diff nodded that it was.

"A man's got to call things according to his own conscience," Ned said as he turned to walk slowly up the hall. "Bad call in some ways, Diff, but I have to respect you for it," he said aloud.

"Those Laman brothers aren't good," the voice from the cell next to him said. Corry's voice had a deep raspy sound due to long periods of disuse. "They would follow me in that truck and yell things out the window. The day before I found the dead lady in the grave, they drove behind me and honked until they almost ran me down. I had to run from them. They took my cart of stuff and put it on their truck and drove away. I found it an hour later up the road and they'd moved things around. Maybe it was them that I saw in the graveyard that night. No, it was someone else."

Diff's hands clenched the bars of his cell. Corry was saying something very important that had to be followed up. There was more to learn here if he could only ask the necessary questions. He automatically felt for the pad that he always carried and found that it was gone. Last night they had taken the pad along with his wallet and other personal possessions when they had booked him. He would not get his things back until he was released.

He searched the holding cell for something to write with. The small cell was eight feet long by six wide and contained a single bunk with a metal frame, narrow mattress, and two army blankets. A toilet and water fountain occupied one end, while the cell door was located at the opposite end. There was nothing available in this small space to write a message to Corry.

The nearest thing to paper in the cell was a roll of toilet paper in a receptacle over the commode. It might be possible to write on that thin tissue if he had something to write with. He frantically searched the cell for any possible implement that could be used to write. For a brief moment he thought of burning wood until it turned to charcoal which could be used to form black block letters. That was a fine idea except there was no wood in the cell and no matches either.

The questions were so important that he'd write the message in blood if he had to.

He would have to. Diff flipped the mattress off its metal frame. He felt along the sides until he found a metal strand that had worked loose from its attachment to the frame. He rapidly worked that small piece back and forth until metal fatigue caused it to snap.

He now held a narrow piece of metal approximately three inches long with one end nearly pointed. He ran the point rapidly back and forth along the rough cement wall until it sharpened.

He took the toilet roll from its receptacle over the commode and placed several sheets in a careful row along the floor. With everything arranged, he held the sharpened metal in one hand, took a deep breath, and jabbed the makeshift needle into his right thumb.

Drops of blood oozed from the cut. He dipped the needle in the blood and wrote on the paper spread on the floor. When the message was complete, he pounded on the wall that separated the cells.

"Huh? What's that? That you, Sarge?"

Diff pounded again.

"No, not the Sarge cuz he's dead. Wait a minute. I'm not in Nam. I'm in Morgan and my head is clear because I'm . . . I'm in jail."

Diff pounded again in the hope this man would climb further back into reality.

"Hey, what's the matter? That you doing the pounding, Diff?"

Diff lay on his side along the wall nearest Corry. He pushed the message through the bottom section of bars and twisted his arm as far to the right toward Corry as he could reach.

"Whatcha doing there, Diff? That's toilet paper in your hand, man. I got some of that stuff in my cell so I don't need yours. You know, those Laman brothers think I'm out of it, but I remember things. I remember you giving me that sleeping bag, Diff. I surely do. Hey, there's writing on that paper. You want me to read that?"

Diff twisted until he could pound on the bottom of the cell wall with his free hand.

"Okay, let me have them," Corry said.

Diff felt the thin paper lifted from his fingers. He pulled his aching arm back in his cell prepared to listen and write another message.

"Hey, man, this looks like it was written in blood," Corry said. "The first one says, 'How long did you sleep in the cemetery?' You want to know how many nights I was sleeping out there, Diff?"

Diff pounded twice on the wall.

"I don't know how long, maybe a couple of nights. Two, three, or something like that, but always in a different grave house, you know. You got more questions? I'm awfully sleepy."

Diff did have more questions, but it would take time to squeeze blood from his finger and write on the thin paper.

"Hi, guys, breakfast time!" Holly said in a cheerful voice.

Diff struggled to his feet and grasped the bars in gratitude. Of all the people in the world he needed to see at this moment, Holly Wilson was the most important. His personal feelings for her and his need to escape from her nearness were put aside. At this moment she was the only person in the world that could help continue Corry's interrogation.

Holly smiled as she put the wicker picnic basket on the floor between the two cells. "You know," she said to Corry, "that these are only temporary holding cells, and Daddy's not equipped for long-term prisoners. I bring meals over whenever we have a sleepover." She laughed at her small joke while she pulled paper plates from the basket and filled them with scrambled eggs, bacon, and toast. She pushed the first one to Corry through his food delivery slot along with a tall Styrofoam cup of coffee.

While Corry wolfed down his breakfast, she moved a bit further down the corridor until she was directly in front of Diff. She filled his plate as she talked to him in a low voice.

"What in the world got into you, attacking those idiots in the middle of the night?" She handed his plate through the bars and looked at him for an answer.

Diff placed his breakfast to one side and made frantic signs to her which said, 'Tell you later. Corry has information for us. The Lamans had possession of his cart for a while. He was in that cemetery for several days and saw people out there where the body was found. Ask him who he saw.'

Holly immediately realized the importance of his signed message and turned to face the other cell. "Hey, Corry, when you were out at the graveyard, you saw others out there, didn't you?"

"Hungry," Corry said through a mouthful of eggs.

"Sure, Corry, I know you are," Holly said. "But you must tell us what else you saw in that crypt."

"People out there," Corry said. "I saw others when the dead woman was there."

"Who?" Holly demanded.

"Sleep now," Corry said.

Several seconds later they heard his deep snores.

"Corry! Hey, Mr. C. Wake up!" Holly yelled through the bars at the sleeping homeless man. "Come on, Corry, it's important!" She finally turned away from that cell to speak with Diff. "It's no use. He's out of it."

'He knows something,' Diff signed to her.

"Darn tooting he does," Holly said. "Daddy's away right now, but I'll get to him the instant he returns and tell him what we've learned so far. He'll agree with us that Corry definitely needs further questioning."

Diff signed his thanks.

Holly reached through the cell bars and gently took his fingers. They stood for a moment with their eyes locked before Diff stepped away and turned his back.

"Well, thanks a heap," Holly said in a hurt voice. "Thanks a real lot." She turned to run down the hall and out the back door as Diff slowly leaned his forehead against the rough concrete of his prison wall.

CHAPTER 9

Diff's body hurt from the fight with the Laman brothers and the final baseball-bat swats administered by Four Eyes. He also ached in a deeper place with a pain that would never heal. His eyes closed as he turned to the wall on his remade bunk, but the picture of her anguished face before she fled from him was vividly clear.

As if a giant hand brushed over him to grant temporary protection for body and mind, a restless sleep finally came peopled with strange and frustrating dreams.

Holly dressed in a long, flowing, white gown was being chased through deep woods by the Laman brothers. From time to time they nearly caught her, but she would wiggle loose and break away. Diff chased the running group, but try as he might to increase his speed, he was not able to close the distance between them. When he finally did draw closer, he found himself in a quicksand whose clutching sludge made it impossible to run. When the others pulled ahead again, he was able to break free but was still not able to catch the taunting brothers as they pursued Holly.

Then, with a surprising final burst of heroic effort, he caught up with the Lamans. He dove for Luke's legs and brought him down while Joe came to his brother's rescue and yelled while he shook Diff.

"Why? Why did you do it!"

Diff's eyes snapped open to see Sheriff Downs bent over his bunk shaking him violently by the shoulders. He tried to sit up, but a deputy pushed him roughly back down on his back.

"Easy, boy," the deputy said. "We don't want to have to put you in chains."

Diff turned to see that the corridor outside the cells was filled with sheriff's deputies and town cops.

"Make way!" someone shouted from the front of the building. "Emergency crew coming!" The cops parted to clear a path for the paramedic ambulance crew to push a hospital gurney down the hall at full speed.

"No need to hurry," Ned Toms said to the ambulance crew in his unmistakably authoritative voice. "He's stone dead, but I don't want him moved until the medical examiner gets here and gives the word."

Diff wondered who they were talking about since he knew full well *he* wasn't dead.

Then the knowledge of who was dead struck him like a physical blow. He rapidly swung his feet off the bunk and broke from the sheriff"s clutches as he drove through the cell door past other deputies and cops who reached for him.

"Get him!" Big Red Downs thundered in his bullhorn-like voice that reverberated throughout the police station. "He's trying to get away!"

Instead of running down the hall in either direction, which would have been the logical escape route, Diff made a right angle turn into Corry's open cell.

It was exactly as he feared. The homeless man lay serenely on his bunk staring at the ceiling with lifeless eyes with a hunting knife stuck in the center of his chest.

He stood over the dead man for a fraction of a second before he was tackled by two large deputies and dumped on the floor. Another cop slapped ankle chains on while a fourth wrenched his wrists behind his back for cuffing.

"Take him to Ray's office for questioning and don't be gentle," Downs bellowed in a voice that would never be mistaken for mellow and soothing.

"Why did you kill him?" Downs shouted in Ray's office while they strapped Diff to a straight chair.

Diff shook his head.

"Don't hand me that dummy bit," the sheriff said. "I know damn well you can talk. Speak up, or do I have to get Deputy Marvel do his special resisting-arrest number on you?"

"What in hell is going on here?" Ray demanded from his office doorway as he pushed into the room. "What in the world are you doing, Sheriff? I go out of town for a couple of hours and you take over my station, my cops, my prisoner, and my office."

"It so happens, you incompetent jerk," Downs said, "that you had a killing in your jail."

"Who are you calling a jerk?" Ray said as he lunged for the sheriff.

"Hold on, Chief," Ned Toms said as he stepped between

the two men. "Knock if off, Downs, and give Ray an apology."

"Okay, sorry about the jerk business, Ray, that was uncalled for, but you did have a killing here and the mayor phoned me. Due to the importance of what happened, he felt that a senior police official should be on hand to start the investigation."

"Will someone please tell me what is going on here?" Ray asked.

"Corry was stabbed to death in his cell, Chief," Ned Toms said. "We think it was done with a hunting knife belonging to Diff."

"How do you know that?"

"Because his name is burned on the wooden handle," Sheriff Downs said.

"So what? Diff has been locked up here since late last night. His apartment could have been broken into by anyone in town while he was locked in here. Then again, anyone can burn a name into any wooden knife handle, so you've got nothing that matters."

"Both cell doors were unlocked, Chief," Ned said.

"Your boy here," Downs said with a gesture toward Diff, "works in this building and has full access to the keys. He could have had a duplicate made and secreted on his body. We figure he picked the fight with the Laman brothers to get thrown in here. When the corridor was quiet, he let himself out of his cell, did a job on the homeless guy, and then went back to his cell to establish an iron-clad alibi. The only problem was that he forgot to relock his own cell door. If he hadn't forgotten that, he would have had a perfect alibi. We found it unlocked when we got here. The facts point to an open-and-shut case. Your friend murdered the model and had to kill Corry to cover it up."

"Orson Ordman, the movie director, once made a feature film called *The Locksmith*," Ned Toms said in his quiet way. "The reviewers said it was a real turkey, but it contained lots of technical details about the mechanics of breaking and entering."

"We still have the evidence of the sleeping bag found with the body that Diff says he gave Corry, and then there's his phony alibi the night Heather Mack disappeared. My money's on murder one for the janitor," the sheriff concluded.

"Diff may not be able to speak," Ray said, "but he is not stupid. You're trying to tell us that not only did he kill a man with a knife that had his own name burned on the handle, but then he also forgot to relock his cell door. You also have not explained how he managed to smuggle a knife in here since he was thoroughly searched when he was booked."

"He works here," Downs snorted. "It was simple enough for him to have had the knife hidden in one of those corridor air vents or someplace like that."

"All the elaborate preparations of hiding knives and getting keys made and yet he uses his own knife and forgets to lock a door. Come on, he'd have to be stoned on something to do dumb things like that."

"Maybe he was," the sheriff replied. "The guy never did look too normal to me anyway."

Ray unlocked Diff's wrists and handed him a pad and pencil. "Tell us what happened, Diff," he said.

Diff began to write, 'Corry spent several nights out at the graveyard and saw something or someone the night Heather was kidnapped. I think he knows . . . knew . . . who killed her. Holly was here early this morning bringing us breakfast, and she also heard part of what Corry had to say. I suggest you ask her for corroboration."

As he ripped off the page and handed it to Ray, Ned Toms took one glance at it and hurried down the hall toward his squad car.

*   *   *

Holly was intently reading a book concerning the unusual hand-signal sign language used by teacher Annie Sullivan with the blind, deaf, and dumb Helen Keller, when the front doorbell rang. Still engrossed in reading, she walked to the screen door and opened it without looking up. "Hi, come on in. I just made some iced tea. Would you care for a glass?" She looked up from her book for the first time and took a step back as she held the door open for the visitor.

"Back inside quick," the visitor said.

"Hey, you've got the wrong season. A ski mask is for winter, not the dog days of summer, and what in the world is that in your hand?"

"Shut up and get back."

"Are you threatening me with that gun?"

"Since I am perfectly serious, it's no threat. I can kill you here and now just as easily as someplace else later. That thing on the end of the pistol is a silencer. Even the people across the street won't hear the sound of the shot."

"This all has to do with the murder of Heather Mack, doesn't it? You are the one, but who are you?"

"You are not terribly bright, are you?" the visitor said with a wave of the gun as duct tape and a pillow case were dumped on the hall table. "Put the tape over your mouth and the sack over your head," were the orders.

"I don't care if you do have a gun, you're out of your living mind if you think I'm going to voluntarily tape my mouth and put my head in something to go somewhere with a murderer," Holly said as she ran for the phone.

"That was not a bright move," the visitor said and followed her through the house. She was caught with the phone in her hand desperately trying to punch in 911. "Nite-nite time" were the last words Holly heard before the gun barrel slammed into the side of her head.

The phone slipped from her numb fingers as her leg muscles lost all controlled feelings and she folded to the floor like a collapsing carton.

*   *   *

'Who else was in the station today?' Diff wrote.

Ray disappeared down the hallway and returned in a few moments carrying the front desk sign-in register. He ran his finger down the list and shook his head in resignation. "It's a who's who of our suspects. The Laman brothers were the first to arrive. The sheriff let them out early this morning on their own recognizance, but their personal belongings were in our safe. They collected their stuff from the desk clerk. After that we had a mass visit by the movie colony contingent: the director, Ordman, was here along with part of his crew consisting of Nell Richards, Tracy Zandt, and Lee Upton. They demanded to see me to obtain permission to leave Morgan for their homes in New York. Since I was out of town, that was obviously impossible."

Diff shook his head in resignation.

Ned Toms walked into Ray's office with a worried frown and body language that shouted resignation and despair. "I think Holly's gone," he announced in a low voice.

Ray gave a noticeable start. "What do you mean, gone?"

"Just what I said, Chief," Toms said. "I went out to your house and when Holly didn't answer I went through the side door which was unlocked. I found the downstairs phone pulled from the wall. I made a quick check and looked in every room and the cellar. I even checked Diff's apartment and the garage. A quick call to the

School for the Deaf indicated she wasn't there. Unless she's out shopping somewhere . . . or do you know anywhere else she might have gone?"

Ray looked thoughtful. "No, I haven't the foggiest. She did our grocery shopping and household errands yesterday, and I understood her plans for the day were to work on a paper she was doing on sign language. She should have been at the computer in her office at the house or else doing research."

"I hate to tell you this, but there were blood splatters on the phone. It looked like it had been yanked from the wall and thrown across the room."

"Check the emergency room!" Ray snapped.

Toms, who usually responded before a command was complete, did not move. "It's been done and negative," he answered quietly.

Diff's waist restraint made a clanking noise as he stood up still attached to the straight chair. He turned toward Ray.

The two men looked at each other for a moment until Ray said, "Find her, Diff. Please."

"That's impossible!" Downs shouted. "That man is a prisoner in a capital murder case. He can't go anywhere except to the county seat in chains."

"I'm releasing him on his own recognizance," Ray said softly, "because right now I need him."

"You have no legal right to do that," the sheriff shouted as he jumped to his feet and turned a deep shade of red.

The eyes of the two senior police officials locked. "I am releasing this prisoner on his word of honor. Do you wish to try and stop me?" Ray said in a steely voice.

The sheriff hesitated and then sat down. "No," he finally said in a low voice. "But if anything happens and he takes off, it's your neck."

Without further command, Ned Toms stepped forward to kneel and undo Diff's ankle cuffs. Then he unlocked the belt restraint and wrists.

"This is very irregular," Sheriff Downs said in a very low voice, "but he is the best tracker we've got."

A minute later Diff and Ray were bending over a geodetic survey map spread across the chief's desk. Sheriff Downs gave low commands over the phone to his deputies. The usually bombastic law officer seemed subdued by the latest turn of events. He was not altogether sure that Diff was innocent, but he knew that the mute man was not involved in the abduction of Holly. His confusion seemed to lower his voice and create a quieter manner.

They all looked up as Sergeant Toms returned to the office with another stricken look on his face. "The bus is gone," he announced. "I'm talking about that rolling luxury home that was parked in our lot. The bus that belonged to the murdered model has been stolen right out from under our noses. A valuable piece of evidence was swiped from a police parking lot."

"I don't think it was stolen at all," Ray said. "I think that some of our movie company people got very impatient with their stay in Morgan and decided to go back to New York in style and comfort while teaching us hicks a lesson. If we block the highway to the Thruway, I'll lay you ten to one we'll find the bus."

"I want an air search mobilized," the sheriff said over the phone. "I want that bus found, and it ought to be easy." He gave a description of the vehicle over the phone and then hung up and turned to face the remainder of the men in the room. "I figure it can't have been gone more than an hour, and so it shouldn't be more than fifty miles from here. It's going to be duck-butter time to find something that large and conspicuous."

"Ten to one it's those crazy movie people, Sheriff. Put your money up," Ray said.

Diff was convinced that this was one bet Ray was going to lose. He didn't think anyone from the movie company had that bus because he believed that whoever killed Corry took the bus and for some strange reason used it in the kidnapping of Holly. Alive or dead, she was in that bus right now.

*   *   *

When Diff was released on his own recognizance, Sergeant Ned Toms drove him back to the Morgan Bar and Grill where he left him next to his battered pickup. There were dents and scrapes along the truck's body and the right front tire had been slashed. The Lamans' truck had already been towed away after they took their last stab of revenge.

Diff changed the tire and started the engine with a great deal of hope and crossed fingers. The front fender whined a cry of protest as soon as he turned the wheel toward the street, but the vehicle was still drivable.

The town and county police were professionals. They would quickly place manned roadblocks at the paved roads on the far sides of Morgan. In the event they had misjudged the time and speed of the stolen bus, the highways would be checked beyond the blockades by the Civil Air Patrol aided by the sheriff department's helicopter. The combination of closure and air surveillance would check all possible traffic in the surrounding area. Diff would take another search approach to close the last possible loophole by flying cross-country to check the obscure dirt logging roads that crisscrossed the forests.

The Morgan Airport consisted of a single runway, a combination office-snack bar, a lone hangar, and an Air Tour office. The manager-pilot of the small facility was Kim Nobel, an attractive brunette of Holly's age who always reminded Diff of Amelia Earhart. When he knocked on the glass panel of her office-radio-room door, she turned with a beaming smile when she recognized him. The door was thrown open as she gave him a bear hug.

"Hey, stranger, why don't you get out here more often? I owe you a couple favors, Diff, and I haven't forgotten what you did to help me get this job."

There was a small blackboard on the wall that contained chalk notations of private flight arrivals and departures. He erased most of the schedule and wrote, 'Holly is missing. We think she's been kidnapped, so I need a flight over and around Bald Mountain and the logging roads.'

"We're practically airborne," Kim said. "What kind of vehicle are we looking for?"

When he wrote, 'A bus,' on the blackboard, her eyes widened.

"A what? Okay, I get it. A bus in the woods is crazy, but we'll look for it, and it shouldn't be hard to find."

The unanswered question was why Holly's kidnapper took the large private bus. It was something that could not just slip away unnoticed. It was very large, people noticed it when it passed by, and it was not the sort of unobtrusive vehicle you would ordinarily use for a getaway from a major crime. That was another unanswered question in a case filled with unanswered questions.

Once aloft, Kim banked over Loon Lake and flew past the edge of town toward the web of narrow dirt roads that crisscrossed the forests that surrounded the town.

The Cessna flew low and could cruise at just under a hundred miles per hour. It was just the right slow speed and low altitude that would allow them to make a thorough search of these remote roads that wound through the woods. Their quarry was a large bus, and although it might be partially hidden by overhanging tree limbs that obscured these paths, it should not be difficult to find from this cruising speed and height.

Kim throttled back the engine to a near-stall speed and flew the single-engine craft in level flight at 500 feet. They decided to fly a ten-square-mile search pattern in grids that worked their way away from the airport and town in sections that overlapped each other. This meant they would have to land once or twice to refuel, and that meant it was going to be a long day. It didn't matter; all that counted was that they find her.

They didn't stop for lunch but ate fruit Diff had foresight enough to grab from the lunch counter when they dashed for the plane. Diff had no appetite since he feared that the longer the delay in locating Holly, the lower her chance for survival. When they did land to refuel, he ran to his pickup to listen to the radio scanner mounted under the dashboard that was tuned to the two local police networks. As various local police and sheriff's department outposts reported, he quickly established that there was no word on Holly or the bus. Their search continued.

Later in the afternoon, Kim signaled that she wanted to make another refueling stop. He grew impatient at the possible time lost and gestured for her to push the small plane to the limit of its range.

Finally Kim turned grimly toward him with lines of disappointment creasing her face. "You know how I think the world of Holly, and she is one of my best friends. I hate to admit it, Diff, but it's not here.

Nothing as large as the bus you described could be hidden on the roads we've flown over today. It is just not here and we have to admit that and realize it's time to call this flight off."

* * *

Diff sat on the leather couch in Ray's office clenching and unclenching his fists, while across the room Ray twirled a pencil until it snapped. It was obvious that both men were perched on the very crest of nervous tension by the way they jumped when the phone rang. Ray snatched up the receiver and snapped a curt, "Yeah, what is it? . . . Oh, for God's sake," he said. "Do I have to bother with that now? Lock them up and throw away the key. . . . Okay, then don't throw the key away, but I want those people in the slammer. Now!"

Diff looked at Ray expectantly waiting an explanation.

"We have more guests," Ray said. "Follow me for the viewing." They trooped down the hall to the holding cells in the rear of the building.

Diff hoped that the next movie Orson Ordman directed was a tragedy since he looked the part as he clenched the bars on the door of the Morgan police station holding cell.

Orson turned away in disgust as Ray and Diff stopped in front of the cells. When he sat on the bunk, his place was taken by Tracy Zandt, who clenched the bars for him. In the next cell Nell Richards and Lee Upton were huddled on that bunk talking in low tones too quiet for anyone else to hear.

Sergeant Toms stood in the hallway with his clipboard, which had recently become part of his daily equipment. "Are you sure you want co-ed holding cells, Chief?" he said with the merest trace of a smile.

"I told you people not to leave town!" Ray shouted at his prisoners. "How dare you try and make it to the city!"

Orson was livid as he leaped to his feet and shook a finger in their direction. "You cannot keep us prisoner here any longer! I have called my lawyer and my Congressman, and I have friends in high places. You Keystone Kops will be security guards at the fire tower on Bald Mountain by the time I'm finished with you."

"How much do you want to wager on your friends getting you out?" Ray said with the first trace of a smile since Holly's disappearance. "Where were they?" he asked Sergeant Toms.

"Deputy Marvel's roadblock stopped them on Route 40 beyond the city limits."

"We were going berry picking," Tracy said with a shrug. "I've always wanted to go berry picking and there aren't many berry bushes in Manhattan."

"This is all Heather's doing," Orson said. "She's reaching back from beyond the grave to torment me. I should have knocked her off years ago."

"What did you say?" Ray snapped.

"He was just running off at the mouth, Chief," Tracy said. "You know how he does that. He didn't really mean that he actually meant to kill her."

"Sure I did," Orson said petulantly.

"Get him out of there! I want a full statement," Ray said.

"Oh, come on, Chief Wilson," Tracy said. "Orson didn't kill anyone. If he wanted Heather removed, he would have ordered me to do it."

"I did and you didn't," Orson said as he glared at her.

The proceedings began to have interest for Nell Richards and Lee Upton in the next cell, and they quit their quiet conversation to approach their cell door.

"We were only going on a picnic, Chief," Nell said with a sweet smile.

"And I was along for the pictures," Lee added.

"I made watercress sandwiches," Tracy threw in.

Even Ordman smiled. "We were planning a maypole dance."

"Oh, get them all out of here," Ray said in disgust. "I can't put up with these people today. Out, and don't try to leave town again until I give permission. Do you hear me?"

CHAPTER 10

Holly stirred and turned over with surprise to find she was sleeping on perfumed satin sheets with a pillow that must have been made of the softest down. As her eyes blinked open, she found herself quite disoriented. She was looking at a wall covered with Venetian blinds painted with a stylized Chinese mountain scene. As she turned her head slightly, she saw an open door leading into a small but elegantly outfitted bath with a full makeup mirror and gold fixtures.

The bedroom was a small but tasteful miniaturized version of a very expensive hotel room. She hadn't the foggiest idea where she was or how she got there. She pressed a hand to her head to feel a very tender lump painful to the touch.

Swirling foggy memories began to slowly focus. She remembered walking to the front door while engrossed in a book. As if a camera lens were slowly being adjusted, her picture-memory began to return until she perceived the vague outline of someone's head covered with a colorful ski mask. Next in focus was the caller's right hand and, even more importantly, the gun clamped in those fingers. She remembered running for the telephone and frantically punching in 911 before something hit her on the side of the head and the blackness closed around her.

Where was she now?

The room began to vibrate as it tilted to one side and then lurched violently in the other direction. With more puzzled realization, she now knew that the room was somehow moving. It took a few more moments to realize that the expensively furnished bedroom with its feminine touches and the swaying movement with its vague background engine sound indicated she was probably on Heather Mack's private bus.

Holly sat up and threw her legs over the side of the bed. The abrupt movement caused dizziness so profound that she was afraid she might faint. After a minute or two the waves of pain began to slowly pass and fade. She looked down at her shorts and felt a strong surge of relief that she might have been put under satin sheets, but at least she was placed there fully dressed.

She pushed open the bedroom door to walk with an awkward swaying movement into the compartment's living-kitchen area. As the bus passed over a very bumpy stretch of road, the jouncing motion increased beyond the shocks' capacity to absorb the punishment. She stumbled and had to grab the edge of the kitchen counter to keep from falling. She worked her way along the counter until she reached the door leading to the driver's compartment, which she tried to open. The brass knob was stiff and immobile, indicating that it was locked from the far side.

She began to pound on the door with both fists.

"Knock it off back there!" a muffled voice shouted in response to her effort.

"Who are you? What do you want?" she screamed.

The door was wrenched open, and she grabbed the side to keep from falling and found herself facing the leering grin of Luke Laman. His brother Joe grimly drove the bus down a dirt fire road with heavy brush growing along each side of the roadway.

"Hi, Little Bo Peep," Luke said.

"You're Big Bo Creep!" she yelled in his face. "Stop this bus immediately and let me off."

"The little lady has come out of it and is fighting mad," Joe said to his brother with a broad grin without removing his eyes from the road.

"I do not believe this," Holly said. "I thought I knew stupid when I saw it, but you guys have really done the trick this time and gone way over the line. Do you realize that you have assaulted and kidnapped me?"

"Come on, Holly," Luke said. "We didn't snatch you. We were only hired as your chauffeur after persons unknown dumped you on the bed back there."

The ruts in the dirt road deepened as they ran over a section that had received damage during a recent heavy storm. The bus lurched from side to side in a violent swaying movement as Joe fought the wheel with both hands to keep the wide vehicle pointed down the narrow winding road.

"Will you run that by me again?" Holly said as she propped herself in the doorway by wedging her hands against the frame.

"Go back and take a nap," Luke said. "Everything will be explained when we get where we're going."

"And where, may I ask, is that?"

Joe Laman gave a high giggle which was an odd sound for a man with three days' stubble of beard, a dirty ponytail protruding from under a cowboy Stetson, and a greasy leather jacket with tarnished brass studs. "That's for us to know and you to find out," he said.

"We'll just see about that," Holly said as she retreated into the passenger compartment and slammed the door. She pulled a stool from under the counter and wedged it under the door handle to keep either of the brothers from breaking in. Surely there had to be an emergency exit in the rear of the bus? Some state law or MVD regulation probably required it—which meant her only problems were to find it and then jump out of a rapidly moving bus in the middle of nowhere.

She began her search and immediately found a round escape and ventilation hatch in the center of the living room ceiling. She pulled a sturdy coffee table into the center of the room.

She stood on the coffee table and reached up to push against the hatch with all her strength. It would only move up a fraction of an inch before it stopped. She imagined that either the Laman brothers or her kidnapper had wedged it shut with something.

She climbed off the table and leaned back on the couch to consider the problem. If the ceiling hatch were sealed, what would happen if the bus turned upside down during an accident? In that event, there had to be another way out as a possible escape route. She continued her search.

At the rear of the bedroom at the back of the bus were the Venetian blinds with the Chinese mountain scene painted on the slats. When she pulled the blinds aside an emergency exit similar to those found in the rear of school buses was revealed. She pushed down on the emergency handle to find that nothing happened. Since there was no play in the bar she realized that it too had been wedged in a closed position.

The bus continued its swaying passage as it rocked down the dirt road at a speed far too fast for such a large vehicle under these circumstances. From time to time when it cornered a sharp curve, it tilted to one side at such a steep angle that Holly was afraid it might go over.

"Hey, little lady," Luke's voice said over an intercom. "You checked it out and see there's no getting away, right?" She heard both brothers give a series of the sharp cruel grunts they passed off as human laughter.

Holly pulled the intercom speaker from its bracket and threw it against the wall to kill the sound of the brothers' grunting-pig laughs.

If at all possible, it seemed as if the bus ride had gotten far worse in the last few minutes. The few windows in the rear living compartment had been blocked so that she could not see where they were. The constant thumping of the wheels against the roadbed made it sound and feel like they were traveling over a highway of fallen trees like the early settlers constructed as corduroy roads.

She knew they would eventually stop and then the brothers would break down the door and come back after her for whatever their purpose. She had no intention of being taken so easily, so she began to plan her attack.

Holly could not be sure how much time elapsed, but she estimated it to be half an hour later when the thumping noise and the dangerous sway of the bus stopped and the engine was shut down. This is it, she thought as the driver's compartment door fell forward toward her with a crash. The brothers had removed the hinges and used their shoulder strength to push it in.

Luke Laman stood in the opening, looking at her with

a wide grin which he punctuated with a couple of pig grunts before he stepped inside the living compartment. All that Holly could see through the windshield behind him was the deep black of total darkness. It was far too early for nightfall, which meant they had a hiding place large enough to hold this huge bus.

"Save some for me," Joe Laman called to his brother.

"I've got plenty for both of you!" Holly shouted as she threw the first bottle directly at Luke's head.

"Hey, Red, cut it out!" Luke cried as a full bottle of spirits bounced off his forehead causing him to stumble backwards into the driver's compartment. "That hurts!"

"What's she doing, bro?" Joe said as he peeked around the corner of the partition at Holly.

"Have one," she said as she threw a liter bottle of Coke directly at Joe. The bottle missed and bounced off the door frame, where it broke and spewed soft drink over both men.

"Hey, knock it off!" Joe yelled back at her.

"We can rip your head off, Red," Luke added.

"Come get more!" Holly said as she stood by the side of the door with the coffee table held over her head.

"Let's rush her," Luke said. "There's two of us and she can't weigh more than a hundred-thirty."

A hundred and twenty seven, Holly said to herself. *And right now I'm losing weight fast,* was her final thought as the brothers shouldered their way into the passenger compartment. Halfway through the doorway they jammed together so tightly that their progress was stopped long enough for Holly to bring the coffee table down over their heads.

Luke Laman dropped straight forward like a falling board. Joe's shoulders and back took the brunt of the blow meant for him, but he still reeled across the room, shaking his head to clear the fog.

Holly darted past them into the driver's compartment. When she reached the door by the passenger side she jammed her hand down on the handle to find that it was tightly locked. She reached across the seat to fumble with the knobs on the console for the switch that would unlock the doors.

A pillowcase was jammed down over her head as the brothers pulled her backwards off the seat into the living area. While she flailed on the floor, Luke held her hands while Joe bound her feet and wrists. When she was securely tied, they propped her up on the sofa and pulled off the pillowcase.

"You sure are a handful," Luke said as he rubbed the bruise on his head.

"Did you guys kill Heather Mack?" Holly demanded.

"Maybe yes and maybe no," Luke said.

"Oh, spare me the games!" Holly said. "I don't think you two are smart enough to have made the model disappear in front of a hundred people including my father," she said.

"Who said we aren't smart?" Joe shot back at her. "That dummy friend of yours who's so smart he can't learn to talk?"

"That man you call a dummy is going to come out here and find me," she said. "And when he does, my father is going to lock you guys up and throw the key away."

"As we speak, your retard friend has been taken care of," Luke said.

Holly felt a quick twinge of terror. Luke spoke as if something had already happened to Diff. That was something she could not even stand to consider. "Exactly what do you mean by that?" she asked softly.

"When we were hired, we told them that Retard would come after us, and since we were coming to the woods, he'd find us. We were told not to worry, that Old Retard would be taken care of," Joe said.

"Shut up!" his brother snapped at him.

"What difference does it make?" Joe snapped back. "Old Red here isn't going anywhere until our friend comes to collect her."

"Collect me for what?" Holly asked.

"Didn't say for what," Luke Laman said. "Our job was to bring the bus and you to this here spot and then to just wait."

"Oh, great," Holly responded. "You stupidos got yourselves involved in a kidnapping to earn a couple of dishonest bucks. Do you know what happens when they catch kidnappers? It's a capital offense, boys. You go to the slammer for life or worse."

"In for a shilling, in for a couple thou," Joe said.

"I don't think it quite goes that way," Holly said with a sigh. "Do you guys know who killed Heather, and if so, how they got away with it?"

"No," both brothers answered together.

"We might make a few slippery bucks here and there but we don't waste pretty ladies," Joe added.

"Then you guys didn't kill Heather?" Holly said.

"We ain't killed no one . . . yet," Joe agreed. "But that doesn't mean we couldn't have been smart enough to make her disappear just like we got you."

"Why me?"

The brothers looked at each other blankly until Luke finally said, "We were paid for a little trip. We were just told to bring you to this spot and wait."

"Who hired you?"

"Don't know," Luke said. "We did our negotiations by phone."

"But we made whoever it is give us two grand up front," Joe said with pride.

"Wait a minute," Holly said. "Are you guys telling me you agreed to participate in a kidnapping over the telephone?"

There was an embarrassed silence until Joe finally said, "Well, we got good up-front money."

"When you find out that the penalty for kidnapping in this state can be the chair, that will come to about twenty-five cents a volt."

More embarrassed silence until Luke said, "Well, it didn't start off like a kidnapping. We were just supposed to snatch this bus and take it out of state and sell it."

Holly shook her head. "You were going to try and fence a bus with gold faucets. Listen, you have the bus, so how about letting me out of here?"

"No can do, Red," Joe said. "I mean, we took good money to bring you here, so we will keep you here. I mean, we have honor, you know."

"Honor you can pretend, but brains upstairs you don't have," Holly said wistfully.

CHAPTER 11

Ray Wilson appeared devastated. He had developed a nervous tic in his right eye, his hands shook, and he seemed to have aged ten years since Holly disappeared. He looked across the desk at Diff with red-rimmed eyes as he slowly shook his head. "I'm not able to come to terms with what might be happening to her at this very moment. You know, Diff, I've been in firefights, both in police work and during Vietnam when I served as an infantry company commander. But my daughter's disappearance is the most difficult thing I have ever had to deal with. I just can't think about the fact that some scumbag has either killed Holly or is doing God only knows what to her."

Diff wanted to yell at his friend with an animal-like rage that announced to the world his determination to find Holly. He wanted to use the force of his will to assure Ray that she was alive at this very moment, and that they would reach her in time to bring her home safely.

Their eyes met, and in that glance Ray seemed to acknowledge Diff's feelings and to draw strength from that determination. "We don't think they got through our roadblocks and made it either to the Canadian border or the Interstates. Kim at the airport assures us that all local planes are accounted for and no outsiders have landed. That means that if she's still alive, she's being held somewhere in Mohawk County."

Ray swiveled in his desk chair to face the large area map mounted on the wall. They both crossed the room to stand before it to look closely at its most prominent features such as Loon Lake, Bald Mountain, and the town of Morgan which was located nearly in the center of the county. Only a few roads led out of the county, and cross-country travel by land vehicle of any sort was difficult because of the mountainous terrain.

Diff wrote a long note that he handed to Ray.

Ray nodded after he read it and then answered, "Yes, we have searched the cemetery, and some of Ned's mountain rescue guys have gone into the sewer system. We've had enough publicity on this situation so that the bus would have been located and reported if it were still in town. It's pretty hard to hide something that size, and we've gone through every building, garage, or structure of any sort large enough to hide the bus. We can't find it, so we think they've still got her in it and must have it hidden on one of the fire roads in the mountains."

Diff composed another note. 'I flew over a good many of those roads and didn't see it.'

"A bus just can't disappear like that," Ray said.

Another note: 'Heather Mack disappeared in front of us, practically the whole police force, and about a hundred others.'

Ray shook his head. "I know. Heather disappeared during

a ten-second blackout. One of the most famous models in the country is filming a commercial in front of a hundred spectators, movie crew, and police, and when the lights go out for a few seconds, she disappears into thin air. Maybe we're up against some mastermind that can out think us, Diff. Since the person who killed Heather is probably the same one that killed Corry and took Holly, maybe we should call in the FBI and the state guys."

Diff knew that if they did that, there would be national television coverage, a massive manhunt would be organized, and Holly, if she were still alive, could count on a life span measured in minutes. He shook his head violently.

Ray's fists pounded the map in frustration. "Where is my daughter?" He sat back behind his desk with his head in his hands. "I can't go on like this. I'm going to the police doctor for a tranquilizer." He reached for the door, but before he left he turned toward Diff with a look of utter anguish on his face. "Find her, Diff. For God's sake, find my daughter."

When he was gone, Diff rolled the desk chair closer to the map and sat examining the outline of Mohawk County. He knew this area well since during the years he had lived in Morgan, he spent nearly every weekend and vacation walking and climbing the hills and mountains of the county. He probably knew the area as well as anyone living.

The phone rang, and thinking it might be Ray with a further thought or instructions, he automatically picked up the receiver and rapped twice on the mouthpiece as a signal that the man who could not speak had picked up the phone.

"Is that you, Diff?" Ned Toms said. Another rap on the mouthpiece told the sergeant that it was. "Okay, then, write a note to the Chief that tells him the Laman brothers have disappeared from the face of the earth. Now, isn't that an amazing coincidence?"

Diff hung up without really mentally processing this information. For the moment it was unimportant what petty crime the Lamans were involved with. The only thing of real importance was finding Holly.

He immediately had second thoughts about the brothers and realized how wrong his assessment was. The Lamans could be extremely important to where Holly was hidden because the brothers were born and raised in Mohawk County and had been hunting these hills as soon as they were large enough to carry a rifle and lantern to jacklight deer. As constant hunters who didn't give a hoot for seasons or licenses, they knew the area well.

The secret was in the map. Where did you hide a thirty-foot-long bus that was nearly too wide to go down the narrow fire and logging roads? If it was still traveling, he would have spotted it from the Cessna. If it was standing still, it was too large to hide in the shadows along the road shoulder. After elimination, that meant that at some point it had been taken off the road.

He searched through Ray's desk drawer until he located the magnifying glass. He returned to the map to examine it more closely. The contour lines that show elevation around the roads would be a good place to begin. He could ignore the regions where the contour lines indicated that the roadside slopes were too steep on either side for the bus to navigate off the road. In certain other places, he knew where the timber would be of such heavy growth that driving such a large vehicle through the dense forest would be impossible. These areas could also be ignored.

He ran the glass over the map surrounding Bald

Mountain. On the far slope beyond the foothills of the mountain, he located a map symbol that he had nearly forgotten.

Diff paused for a moment deep in thought and then followed the line carefully as it ran toward Bald Mountain.

The knowledge erupted like sun bursting through a hazy cloud layer. He knew where the bus was hidden! He knew why it could not be seen from the air. This meant he now knew where Holly was held prisoner . . . if she were still alive, he would find her.

The desk chair slammed against the wall as Diff dashed for the parking lot.

*   *   *

"Let's be civilized about this," Holly said to the Laman brothers. "You untie me, turn the bus around, take me home, and we won't mention this to my father."

"Turn it around!" Luke laughed a half dozen pig grunts. "You have to be kidding. We can't do that because it's impossible. You don't know where you are, do you?"

"I know we're somewhere near Bald Mountain," Holly answered.

"You know, we got a full kitchen in this thing," Luke said. "And I checked the freezer and found there's some dandy steaks in there that we could chow down on. How about it, Red?"

"How about what?"

"Making like a cooky. You know, whipping us up a good, old-fashioned, home-cooked meal and then maybe later we can party a little."

"You guys have to be kidding!" Holly said and then thought better of the flip remark. It might be the better part of valor to cook for these idiots and feed the animals rather than have their party begin immediately with her as the door prize. "You know, now that you mention it, I'm kinda a little hungry myself," she said. "There's nothing like a knock on the head and a good kidnapping to really work up an appetite for you."

Joe gave Luke a poke in the ribs with his elbow. "Isn't she a cutie, bro? Now, this Red has a real sense of humor and I bet she can cook up a storm."

"Sure I can," Holly said. "Untie me, point me at those steaks, and we'll get things going."

The brothers looked at each other with uncertain glances until Luke shrugged. "Untie her. She can't get out of here to go anyplace."

The brothers compromised and untied her hands but left her legs in a loose hobble. Holly staggered toward the kitchen area and freezer knowing she was going to move in slow motion. The longer this meal took, the better her chance of survival.

*   *   *

Diff drove his pickup down the Bald Mountain fire road toward the railway cut. He drove with one hand while the other flipped open the double-barrelled .12-gauge shotgun to check that it held a double load of deer shot. Satisfied, he closed the chamber with a flick of his wrist and heard the satisfying click as the weapon snapped into place. He placed the gun by his side and made sure he had extra shells in his pocket. He pressed down on the gas and used both hands to fight the steering wheel as he increased speed to careen down the fire road as fast as he could and still hold the road.

Churning around in the back of his mind was the nagging fear that he might be too late. It was always possible that Holly's abductor had already killed her and tossed the lifeless body into the brush by the side of the road. The only relief he had from this fear was the thought that if he wanted her dead quickly, why hadn't it been done at the house rather than an elaborate kidnap scenario in such a conspicuous vehicle like the luxurious bus?

Decades ago the land in this area had belonged to a very large paper company. That corporation had cut timber on the foothills and either floated the logs down the river or carried lumber out on the short railroad line they had constructed to connect with the main line. The property had eventually been purchased by the state as a wilderness preserve and all lumbering had ceased.

Diff slammed on the brakes when he realized that he'd missed the cutoff. The truck's rear wheels locked as he slewed back and forth across the road in a skid that nearly dumped him in the brush. He regained control of the truck and did a four-point U-turn to return the way he came. A quarter of a mile back was the entrance to the rail line hidden from view by a lush third-generation growth of timber and brush. When the railroad had been abandoned by the paper company, they had only ripped up those portions of track that crossed roads or private property. The remainder of the roadbed had been left intact to rust away in the forest.

In his hikes through the woods Diff had often crossed and recrossed the line. Although it was hidden from view from the air due to its narrow gauge and the growth of overhanging trees, most of the line was still faintly visible under a layer of weeds and forest litter.

The pickup reached the point where the tracks had once crossed the fire road. Diff turned his truck violently to the right and smashed his way through a light growth of brush and saplings. When he reached the tracks a few yards from the roadbed, his wheels began to jounce over the rail ties still in place. The pickup was able to continue its forward motion although the ride was giving his shocks and suspension system a terrible beating.

After a half mile he saw the entrance to the tunnel that went under Bald Mountain. Ordinarily its entrance was hidden from view by forest growth, so it was obvious from snapped branches and bruised limbs that something large had recently rammed its way into the tunnel.

It was a perfect place to hide a bus. He was somewhat surprised that the kidnapper hadn't returned to the entrance to camouflage the tunnel once he had the vehicle inside. Perhaps he intended to do that when he finally abandoned it. With brush pulled across the entrance, it might be years before the bus was discovered. The fact that he had not camouflaged the entrance might mean that Holly and her captor were still inside.

Diff immediately cut his engine and quietly left the pickup, carrying the shotgun. He cautiously entered the tunnel and stood crouched against the wall for several minutes while his eyes adjusted to the dark.

As his night vision increased, he was able to see the rear of the bus parked a hundred feet inside the tunnel. He moved slowly toward it in a manner that kept his back against the dank tunnel wall and the shotgun pointed ahead.

When he reached the bus, he ran a hand over the rear emergency door until touch told him that it had been chained shut and padlocked. He held the shotgun with both hands as he squatted to peer under the bus. There were no legs silhouetted in the light that spilled through the front windshield. No one seemed to be standing in the tunnel, but he could hear faint steps inside the bus.

He moved slowly along the tunnel wall near the side of the bus until he reached the front. He ducked so he wouldn't be visible through the windshield as he moved across the nose of the vehicle.

"Hey, Red, you are something," he heard the unmistakable voice of Luke Laman say.

What in the world was going on? It almost sounded like a party, he thought.

"Hey, this steak is great," Joe Laman said. "How about seconds?"

"Coming up as soon as I throw two more on the grill," Holly said gaily. "More wine, boys?"

"You know it," Luke answered. "I always thought wine was for pussycats, but it's not bad drinking."

Diff peeked over the edge of the windshield to look past the driver's compartment through the open door into the traveling compartment. He saw the Lamans sitting at a table set with what appeared to be good crystal and fine bone china. The brothers ignored the niceties of the table settings as they each held T-bone steaks with their fingers. They were attacking the meat like starving wild dogs. Holly stood nearby with a half-empty wine bottle in her hand, looking at them with a look that was a mixture of mild disdain tempered with fright and concern.

Diff found the strange homey scene confusing, but he didn't have time to dwell on what was happening—the only important fact was that Holly was alive and needed help.

*   *   *

Luke Laman belched and Joe's response was another pig laugh.

Holly wondered if she could convince these guys to eat a third steak or drink a couple more bottles of wine. She certainly hoped so, because otherwise she had the feeling that time was running out. The Lamans' food consumption was beginning to slow, and from time to time they eyed her as if she were dessert, which she suspected that she very well might be.

Luke pushed back from the table with another burp. "Got to tell you, Red, that bro and I flipped a coin and I won. You are one lucky girl."

Holly's hand brushed against the steak knife hidden in the waistband of her shorts. She had the feeling that since she would only be able to get one of the brothers, Luke had really lost.

It was Joe Laman's turn to push back from the table. "Well, Luke, get on with it. Move it, man!"

Luke's smile was closer to a leer, but it seemed to be the best he had. Holly stepped back until she struck the side of the bus. She pulled the steak knife from her waistband and waved it in front of her. "Either of you guys touch me and I use this."

The brothers gave their grunting laughs as Joe's foot lashed out and neatly kicked the small knife from her hand with such force that it clattered against the ceiling.

Holly turned in preparation for the dash to the driver's compartment with the hope that this time she might get the door open.

"Come on, Red, we don't mean dirty stuff," Luke said. "I get to thank you for the good feed, that's all."

There was a wrenching sound of protesting metal from the roof of the bus. As they looked toward the ceiling, the emergency hatch was torn open and Diff dropped into the room to land on the table with enough force to break it in half and shatter a good deal of glassware and china.

He swung the shotgun with sufficient force to send Luke sprawling when the barrel caught him on the shoulder. A deafening blast from the shotgun sprayed the ceiling, which caused the brothers to immediately raise their hands over their heads.

"Well, look who just dropped in," Holly said gleefully before she yelled at the top of her voice. "Take the position! Lamans, you know what I mean. You've had plenty of experience in police searches. Take the position, now!"

The brothers automatically put the palms of their hands on the wall, spread their legs apart and leaned down in standard police-search position. Diff handed the shotgun to Holly as he expertly patted the Lamans for weapons. He found that each carried a switchblade knife. Joe also had a razor-sharp box opener, while Luke had a can of mace for added protection.

The weapons made a neat little pile at the far end of the coach interior. Diff nodded at Holly as he held up handfuls of crisp new hundred-dollar bills taken from each brother's pockets.

"Question time!" she snapped out. "Who hired you two to bring me out here?"

No answer. Diff shook his head for a repeat of the question.

"I mean business," Holly said. "Who hired you two lunkheads? Or do you want a double barrel of deer shot in your rear?"

Luke gave a pig laugh. "You wouldn't do that."

"I don't know," Joe protested. "We're stuck way out here and no one would ever know, so she just might."

"Maybe you're right," Luke agreed. "Okay, Red, to answer your question. We told you before that we was contacted by phone. Someone asked if we wanted to make a quick couple of thou. Of course, I said yes. I mean, who isn't for making a quick two thou for a little work?"

"Man or woman's voice?" Holly immediately shot back.

"Don't know. The voice was kinda funny sounding like it was coming over one of those squawk-box things. You know what I mean? One time I swore it was a guy, another time it was like a woman. I don't know."

"Are you telling us that you committed a felony for someone, and you don't even know if it was man or woman?"

The brothers did not answer.

"Didn't you realize you were kidnapping me?"

"Nope," Luke answered. "The voice told us where to pick up the bus and said the money would be in an envelope under the seat and a young woman would be sleeping in the back. We were to drive you out here and wait until they came for you. It was made out like it was one of those practical jokes some people play."

"Most tricks don't involve taking people places against their will," she said.

"Yeah," both brothers exclaimed simultaneously.

"So someone paid you for a couple of hours of bus driving?"

There wasn't any answer to that one but the brothers tried. "We figured it was one of those movie people who was working on a story for a movie," Joe said. "He wanted to see if two guys could get away with a bus."

Diff shook his head.

"With me in it?" Holly said.

"To check on the cops," Luke suggested. "To see how long it took them to find us."

"And they start by knocking out the Chief's daughter?" Holly added. "Cut it out, you guys!"

Diff wondered why the killer wanted Holly kept alive. The question was answered by an explosion and a sheet of flame that flared up in front of the bus.

Flames engulfed the front of the bus to such an extent that it would be impossible to get out the doors in the driver's compartment. Diff realized that someone had thrown a gasoline bomb at them.

There was another explosion at the rear of the bus. The first firebomb was to seal them in the bus while the second was meant to ignite the gas tank.

There were now two more distant explosions—one to the front and a closer one at the rear. These were followed by a series of rock falls which meant both ends of the tunnel were now sealed with falling debris.

This unused rail tunnel was to be their eternal tomb.

CHAPTER 12

"The doors are jammed!" Luke Laman yelled in terror. "We can't get out! We're trapped in here and the whole thing is going to blow any second."

"Someone break the windshield!" his brother screamed.

"With what?" Luke yelled back.

"Use your head if you have to, dummy!" the nearly hysterical Joe shot back.

While the brothers continued arguing, Diff gave Holly a boost to grab the rim of the ceiling emergency exit. He hoped that neither brother came up with a way to break through the front windshield as that would probably cause an immediate backdraft of flame into the bus interior that would instantly incinerate them. He gave Holly a final shove through the opening and then jumped to grab the edge and pull himself up. They slid along the bus roof and hand in hand jumped to the roadbed.

"Hey, they went out through the roof!" Luke Laman screeched at his brother.

"Let's go!" Joe yelled as he pushed his brother aside in order to be next through the exit.

The bus lights were still lit although the firebomb had created a spider web of fractures over the front windshield. The bus lights along with the flames allowed them to see through the smoke toward both ends of the tunnel. Dynamite charges planted there had been effective and caused part of the tunnel roof to collapse and seal them in this very long grave.

"We're trapped in here to die like rats," Luke said with an edge of deep fright in his voice. "The bus is going to blow any second and that will kill us."

"Do something, Diff," Joe Laman begged.

"Boy, you guys are something," Holly said. "For years you've been calling him Retard and now you expect him to save your rotten lives. You guys are all heart."

The fire increased in intensity as the first of a series of small fireballs burst from the engine. In minutes, flame and heat would reach the gasoline tank and cause an explosion which in the sealed tunnel would spell their doom.

Diff watched flame tongues spiral toward the ceiling of the tunnel as if sucked by a powerful updraft. The rise of fire and smoke created a chimney-like appearance as if they were trapped inside a fireplace with a good draw. He realized that the reason for the fire's upward passage was the existence of some type of vent. There must be a ventilator shaft above them that ordinarily brought clean air into the tunnel from the slopes of Bald Mountain, but which was now sucking up smoke and flames.

Without further hesitation, Diff took Holly's hand to indicate that she should follow him. He climbed back to the top of the bus using the ladder that ran to the exterior luggage rack.

"You're onto something," she said and coughed.

He pointed at metal ladder rungs embedded in the side of the tunnel. The ladder was partially obscured by smoke, but it was clear that it ran straight up to the ceiling and then disappeared in the darkness over their heads.

"A ventilator shaft," she coughed in amazement. "It's filled with smoke. Do you think we can make it?"

He shook his head to signify yes. They would have to make it, he thought, for it was their only chance. Without waiting for a further response, he jumped for the nearest metal rung and pulled himself up to reach for the next one. Hand over hand Diff climbed up the wall of the tunnel into the narrow shaft over their heads.

Holly, followed by the Laman brothers, climbed after him.

As they emerged from the tunnel roof into the body of the narrow air shaft, the volume of heat and smoke increased. The shaft was acting as a perfect chimney and was drawing smoke from the burning bus into its chamber. They were quickly surrounded by smoke and began to cough and choke on the foul air.

Holding his breath to keep from breathing the polluted air, Diff hoped they had built this tunnel near the rim of the mountain rather than straight through the center. He knew that if they had to climb this shaft to the top of the mountain, it would be too far for them to go without breathing clean air. He continued climbing with the hope that it wasn't much farther and that Holly was able to follow.

The smoke parted for a brief moment which allowed Diff to see bright light ahead. Seconds later he was clear of the shaft and in the open air on the side of the mountain. He rolled over the rim and away from the shaft where he lay gasping for breath.

Holly, her face streaked with cinders, came out of the tunnel to roll after him until they bumped together. Their arms automatically went around each other in an embrace that was filled with joy and elation at their survival.

"Look at that," Luke said through a coughing fit as his brother came out of the shaft behind him. "I always told you that Retard and Red were a real close couple."

Diff snapped his hands away from Holly's body and stood in embarrassment. Holly sat up to hug her knees and look at him with a face filled with unasked questions. He realized that he had taken advantage of her and the situation. He wanted to tell her how sorry he was, but he couldn't. In place of an unspoken apology, he turned to walk down the hill toward his pickup.

With a loud roar a column of flame shut up the ventilation shaft as the bus exploded in the tunnel.

*   *   *

When Diff drove into the police station parking lot, men and women poured from the building. Not only were town and county cops present, but numerous city workers and friends of the Wilsons had come for the vigil. Sergeant Toms climbed into the truck bed to talk in a low voice with the Laman brothers.

Ray Wilson came slowly out of the door and stood watching the activities with a serious look that gradually changed to a beaming smile as he saw his soot-streaked daughter climb unharmed from the truck. He walked slowly over to her where Holly gave him a very big hug.

He held her for a moment before he reached over to shake Diff's hand. "Thanks," was all his choked voice was able to say.

With his arm around his daughter, Ray walked back in the building and down the hall to his office. He was followed by Diff and Sergeant Toms with the Lamans. When he sat behind his desk, he seemed to have recovered his mental balance now that he knew his daughter was safe. His voice resumed most of its old authority. "Will somebody tell me what's going on?" he ordered with the return of his sense of command.

"Diff found me in the bus," Holly said.

"I figured that," Ray said. "I hope you are not going to tell me that the shoplifting Lamans, heretofore not known as master criminals, were responsible for the murders of Heather Mack and Corry, and for snatching you?"

When Holly hesitated, Sergeant Toms spoke in his quiet manner. "It would seem to me that it should be noted for the record that the boys came along peacefully. They were sitting in the back of the pickup without handcuffs as if they were being driven to a church picnic rather than facing a long stretch in max security."

"What about the damage the Retar—I mean Diff—did to our truck?" Luke said even when poked in the ribs by his brother.

"They don't allow many pickup trucks in max security," Toms announced.

"By the time you guys get out, pickups will be as old as the pony express because everyone will have a private helicopter," Ray said. "Although it is interesting that you came along so peacefully. Either of you two care to explain that sheep-in-wolf's-clothing attitude?"

"Holly made us promise no funny business," Luke said in a voice that hardly anyone could hear.

"What promise did she make to keep you guys from jumping out of the truck?" Ray pressed.

"She said the Retard, I mean Diff, would track us down if we did and it would go real hard on us."

"That's still not answering my question. You know you boys are facing serious time here?"

"No, Daddy," Holly broke in. She swallowed hard before she continued at a very fast rate, "The Lamans helped rescue me and had nothing to do with the other crimes."

No one in the room was more surprised at this statement than the brothers who looked at her with wide-eyed amazement.

"Holly, your nose is getting longer," her father said with a facial expression that was a cross between amusement and concern.

"It's only growing a teeny bit, Daddy. I was kidnapped, but these guys didn't do it. They were more like my chauffeurs, and I refuse to press charges for their stupidly trying to earn a few dishonest dollars."

The brothers, who had discussed how much time they were going to serve all the way back to town, assumed facial attitudes usually seen on men applying for the priesthood.

Ray and Ned Toms looked at Diff for an opinion.

Diff shrugged and gave a half smile at Holly. It was her choice, was his unspoken answer.

"For the time being, I'm going to let the matter of the brothers drop," Ray said. "Now will you tell me what happened out there?"

Holly began to tell of the events that occurred from the time she answered the door at the house until their escape from the railway tunnel. When she finished, her father tapped his pencil on the desk blotter. "It would seem that whoever attacked you in our home is the killer. The question is, who was it?"

The room was silent and even the Laman brothers seemed profoundly interested in her answer.

"I . . . I don't know," Holly said. "I'm not fudging on that one. I remember answering the door and finding someone wearing a ski mask. I ran back to the phone. Then everything went blank until I woke up in the bed on the bus."

"Oh, great," Ray said. "We're inches away from the solution to this crime and you didn't see a face and the rocket scientist brothers made a deal over the phone. But why all this elaborate business with the bus? Why would anyone go to all the trouble of hiring the Lamans to take the bus into the tunnel and then blocking the escape routes to kill you all? It would have been simpler if he had killed you right away at the house. Thank God that didn't happen. But why steal a bus which is a hard thing to hide, have it driven into the tunnel, and then have to go to the difficulty of blowing the tunnel at both ends? It doesn't make sense."

Diff wrote on a legal pad while Ray spoke. He flipped the pad around so that Ray could read what he had written.

"Diff says that the bus must have contained an important clue and therefore had to be destroyed," Ray read. "He also believes the killers thought that with Holly dead and Diff arrested for Corry's murder, the trail of clues would be eliminated. It was necessary that both be silenced because they had both talked to Corry in the holding cell. The killers did not know how much Corry had actually seen or told Diff and Holly, but they couldn't be sure, so Holly had to die and Diff had to be completely discredited. Okay, that makes sense, but remember that we went over that bus with a fine-tooth comb when it was parked in our lot. We did not find anything that remotely resembled a clue."

Diff didn't know the answer to that question, but as he looked over at Holly and the Laman brothers, he did know that all four of them were filthy. The tunnel explosions and the escape through the ventilation tunnel filled with smoke and soot made them look like 19th-century chimney sweeps.

Holly understood his look. "Before we do more thinking about this stuff, I suggest long showers."

Diff nodded in agreement and started for the door after Holly and was followed by the Laman brothers. Holly laughed and poked Luke in the chest with her finger. "We four do not a family make. I suggest that you two go scrub down at your usual place, the men's room at the Morgan Bar and Grill."

After Diff showered and was toweling off in front of the bathroom mirror, he stopped stock still and stared at his reflection. He dropped the towel and slowly opened the front of the medicine chest and swung the mirror door slowly back and forth. *Things are not always what they seem*, he thought and then slammed the mirror shut.

He dashed for his bedroom to throw on clothes. He knew how Heather Mack had disappeared in front of a hundred onlookers. If his theory was correct, he also knew what important clue had been in the bus before it blew.

*   *   *

"Where are we going?" Holly asked as Diff drove the pickup through town.

He had already written the note that he now handed to her.

"'The Idle Hours Motel,'" she read.

He nodded as she continued, "For some reason you want to search Lee Upton's motel room?" He nodded again. "You think that those pictures he took of the movie filming the night Heather disappeared might provide a clue as to who did it and how?"

Diff nodded again as he turned in the drive to the motel and drove to the rear. He decided to park away from the building and leave the truck in the shadows a dozen yards behind the units.

He reached down to where he ordinarily kept the shotgun and couldn't find it. It took a few seconds to realize that he had taken the weapon into the rail tunnel and left it on the bus during the fire. They would have to make the search without the protection of a weapon, but since rumor had it that Lee and Nell Richards usually stayed together, the room should be empty and safe.

After making sure that Lee's room was not occupied, Diff pried open a small window in the rear that entered into that unit's bathroom. He gave Holly a boost inside and then went around to the room's front door as she opened it from the inside. He slipped in and quietly closed the door.

The pictures were in the identical location they were in the first time they had been in the room with Lee. He had shot dozens of still pictures on Heather's last night and taped the proofs in neat rows over a rear wall.

After making certain the blinds were drawn, Diff removed the shade from a brass bedside lamp. The cord was sufficient to reach to the wall where the pictures were taped, and the naked bulb provided the bright illumination a close examination required.

"I wish I knew what we were looking for," Holly said as she started at one corner to examine each photo carefully and worked her way along the rows.

Diff found a magnifying glass on the bureau top which was covered with cameras, extra lenses of all shapes and sizes, and a host of other photographic equipment. He started at the opposite side from Holly and examined each picture closely with the magnifying glass in one hand and the lamp in the other.

They met in the center of the wall where the photo proofs seemed to have been taken immediately before and right after the blackout.

Diff noticed that the row of pictures on the right row was a before series depicting Heather in her hoop skirt either standing on her mark or walking to her place. In either event she was always in front of the other models and town extras who were all dressed in period costumes or hooded capes. Holly was easily recognizable because her hood was thrown back to reveal her vivid red-gold hair.

Diff examined the set of pictures on the left for the third time. These shots were taken immediately after the model's disappearance and showed an empty hoop skirt in a pool on the ground on top of Heather's mark. These pictures also revealed everyone's gradual realization that the star of the filming had somehow disappeared.

He knew how Heather Mack had vanished and the photographs proved it.

Diff sat at the motel room's small desk to hastily write a note to Holly in large block letters. She stood over his shoulder and grabbed each scrawled page as soon as it was complete. When she had finished reading the last one, she went back to the wall of pictures and bent to take another look at the ones Diff had examined last.

"'Look at the group shot before the blackout and notice the caped figures in the background, particularly the ones standing behind and to the side of Nell Richards,'" Holly read aloud. "Okay, I did that." Then she read, "'Now look at the same group photographed almost immediately after the lights went back on again.'" Holly took another look and then read the remainder of the note. "'Now count both groups,'" Diff had written.

"Okay," she announced, "I've done that and count six caped ladies in group one before the blackout . . . and seven afterwards . . ." She turned to him in amazement. "So that's how it was done?"

The sharp zip of the silenced pistol shot was the only sound they heard. The top of the shadeless table lamp shattered as its bulb and fixture exploded under the bullet's impact. The remains of the brass lamp fell to the rug sputtering and spewing sparks in a circle like a fireworks sparkler.

"Heather thought it was all one big joke . . . in the beginning," Lee Upton said from the doorway. He slammed the outside door as they whirled to face him and the automatic pistol with the long silencer on the end of its barrel clenched in his hand.

"I told her it was only a practical joke to get on Orson's nerves," Nell Richards said from Lee's side. "I carried the extra cape under mine until the lights went out. As soon as it was dark, Heather stepped out of her hoop skirt and put on the cape. She joined the rest of us at the rear of the stage and pulled the hood across most of her face. After the search had finished, we sneaked her back on her bus. Along about then, she was ready to burst back on the scene with a laugh and tell everyone that the joke was over. Of course, we couldn't allow her to do that, so we had to quiet her down. At the very end she knew it wasn't any joke, but by then it was too late—far too late. I just thought I'd let you two know before Lee kills you," Nell concluded.

"Then there was a clue on the bus and that's why you had to destroy it," Holly said.

"But of course," Nell said. "Foolishly we left the extra hooded cape on the bus. Someone would have gone through the bus again and found the cape. That person might have put the whole thing together like Diff just did without the cape. So, bus and cape had to be destroyed, just as you two have to be eliminated."

"You firebombed the bus with us inside?" Holly said.

"Yes, you got away that time," Lee said, "but it's highly doubtful that you'll pull off another lucky escape."

With his eyes wide in fear Diff put his hands to his face. His fingers seemed possessed with a life of their own as they wiggled over his cheeks.

"The mute coward has lost it," Lee said as he pulled the slide back on the pistol and let it slam forward. "He needs to be put out of his misery."

Diff's fingers sent a sign message to Holly: 'You are nearest the broken lamp. Grab it and Lee's ankle.'

With only precious seconds left, Holly did not take time to consider or evaluate his request. Although her keen intelligence made her aware of the consequences, she did not hesitate.

"Oh," Holly groaned as her eyes rolled back in her head. "Please, help me," she managed to gasp before she fell straight forward to the floor where she grabbed the base of the shortcircuited lamp with one hand and Lee's ankle with the other.

"They're both such cowards," Nell managed to mutter as Lee Upton went into electrical shock convulsions. His fingers holding the pistol went into spasms caused by the electrical charge and discharged its bullets at the ceiling as he fell.

"Lee!" Nell Richards screamed as she reached for her lover with both hands. As soon as physical contact was made, she went into shock. The three people on the floor writhed in waves of electrical current.

Diff threw himself across the room directly toward the lamp's plug which he pulled from the wall.

With the electrical current shut off, the thrashing bodies stopped moving as a distant police siren pulled nearer.

CHAPTER
13

They sat on the wide veranda at the house on the hill while Holly, with a surgical bandage across her broken nose, served iced tea. From time to time her father glanced lovingly at her as if to assure himself that she was still well and whole.

The porch swing creaked under the weight of Sheriff Downs, who casually rocked with half-closed eyes. He yawned and looked up lazily to take a tall glass of tea from Holly. "Thank you, ma'am, much obliged. Hope your nose is better, but you were lucky to go through all that and only end up with a busted nose from your fall to the lamp."

Sergeant Ned Toms sipped tea while he made notes on his constantly present clipboard.

Diff sat on the floor with his back against a porch post. He was able to see Holly from the corner of his eye without looking directly at her. He considered the fact that yesterday she had nearly given her life for him without hesitation. Although he knew at the time she was young and healthy, submitting her to electrical voltage under those circumstances could have been disastrous.

He would never forgive himself for placing her in such jeopardy. He objectively knew that for the plan to work, the person nearest the broken lamp had to be the one to grab it. He still had no right to place her in such danger when he might have leaped at Lee to fight for the gun. Logic told him that he probably would have been shot in the attempt, which wouldn't have helped Holly since the gun would have been turned on her next. He knew in his heart that what they did was their only hope, but that didn't remove his guilt.

All of this was one more reason requiring him to leave within the hour. The things he needed to take with him were still stowed away in the back of his pickup parked not thirty feet away

"Well, that about wraps it up except for our final statements to the prosector," Ned Toms said as he put the clipboard aside and methodically packed his pipe with an aromatic tobacco mixture.

"How can you continue smoking after all the studies that have been published?" Holly said as she passed him a plate of warm tollhouse cookies.

"I'm quitting tomorrow," Toms replied in his slow, measured manner as he puffed contentedly on the pipe.

"Uh-huh," Ray said. "You've been giving us that tomorrow business for five years."

"Did you tell the sheriff about our discovery of Lee's latest pictures?" Toms said in an attempt to change the subject.

"You'll find this hard to believe, Sheriff," Ray said, "but Lee Upton actually took a photograph of Nell Richards shooting Heather Mack. We not only have his statement, but we have the actual commission of the crime recorded on film. The guy was such an obsessive fiend at snapping pictures that he couldn't resist recording the actual murder. Those two are turning against each other like a cobra and a mongoose."

The swing groaned as Big Red Downs increased the speed of his movement. "That's going to make the prosecution's job a lot easier. You know, Chief," he said to Ray, "I can understand your letting the other movie people go home, but you did astound me and a lot of other people in town when you released those no-account Laman brothers. You could have nailed them on half a dozen charges and the whole county would have been better off when our petty-crime rate dropped in half."

"Let's just say the brothers made a rather unusual plea bargain that gives them a sentence far worse than our county lockup or the state penitentiary," Ray said.

"I'd call it cruel and unusual punishment, which I might point out is against the Constitution," Ned Toms said as he blew perfect smoke rings contemplatively into the air over their heads.

"Here comes the judge and executioner with her prisoners," Holly said as she pointed down the street. The Laman brothers' pickup truck slowly approached them with a great deal of loud clanking and clattering from its mutilated chassis.

"I do not believe what I am seeing," the sheriff said as his mouth dropped open. "Which one is it? I mean, which brother is the daddy?"

"From what Sally told me, it can be whichever one

she wants," Holly said. "I think they come as a matched pair, although personally I'd take Luke as marginally better of the two."

The battered pickup stopped at the edge of the drive with Luke Laman behind the wheel and his brother Joe Laman on the passenger side. Sally Way was sitting between them smiling broadly; the brothers were not. The door on the passenger side opened as Joe got out and turned to help the astonishingly pregnant Sally climb down.

"I'd like you to be maid of honor, Holly," Sally said as she waddled toward them with a Cheshire cat-like grin.

"Do you really plan to go through with a formal wedding even though it might take place in the hospital delivery room?" Holly asked in amazement. "I would have thought a simple family ceremony immediately, if not sooner, might be in order."

"Who's the lucky man, Miss Sally?" Ray asked, trying to hide behind a brave attempt not to smile.

Sally turned to face her two companions who were five paces behind her. The force of her look caused the brothers to take an automatic step back.

Luke peeked around the young woman's increasing girth. "No charges are going to be filed against us, right, Chief?"

Ray bit his lip to choke back the laughs that lurked just beneath the surface and fought to erupt in whooping yelps. "Well now, Luke, I wouldn't force a man into anything that wasn't of his own doing stemming from free choice. I assume this is your decision, right?" The brothers nodded in unison. "Okay, then, just let me say that I believe in the sacredness of the family, and that's why I think you should stay here in Morgan with your wife-to-be and coming child rather than serve time. I assume you are the winner, right?"

"The winner or looser, depending on how you look at it, gets to be best man," Ned Toms said with a rapid series of pipe puffs that indicated that he too was fighting a gleeful impulse to laugh.

"Come on, Sally," Holly called. "Don't keep us in suspense any longer. Who's the lucky man?"

By the look on their faces, Diff wasn't exactly sure the brothers considered the final choice as a lucky selection so much as a punishment sentence. The truth of the matter was, considering all the parties involved, no one was exactly sure who the father was, and in the case of brothers, DNA testing would not be conclusive.

Sally pointed to one brother and then the other as if choosing sides for a pickup basketball game. Her finger paused in front of one Laman and then switched to the next one. "Luke!" she finally screeched as she threw her arms around him. "My baby's daddy!"

"Congratulations, bro," a very happy Joe Laman said as he waved good-bye to those on the porch and got behind the wheel of the pickup. He coaxed the truck engine to life as Sally and her fiancé joined him on the front seat.

"There's a job opening down at the convenience store, and another one at the fertilizer factory," Ned Toms called after them as the truck drove away.

As soon as the truck passed out of sight, there was a strange silence on the porch until everyone's self control disappeared to be replaced by gleeful rocking laughter.

"Lordy, lordy," Big Red Downs said. "Sally might make respectable citizens of those brothers yet." The laughter finally died away as Ned Toms returned to his clipboard. "Let's wrap this up and finish off this case because I'm still curious about a couple of details," the sheriff continued. "What did Nell Richards stand to gain by getting rid of Heather Mack?"

"Fame and fortune," Ray said. "You saw how quickly the director used her to replace Heather. With Heather gone, Nell was assured of a bright and shining career."

"And Lee Upton went along with her plan because he was bonkers over her," Downs added.

"That's about the size of it," Ray said as the large sheriff resumed his slow swinging. "Of course, he also had economic interests. With Nell famous, the value of his photographs and his intimate exclusive shots of her increased in value."

"Another question," Downs asked. "The Laman brothers had possession of Corry's cart for a time after they took it from the homeless man. Are they the ones who planted the evidence in the cart? If so, Sally's baby or not, they should be charged accordingly."

"That's not the way it came down," Ray said. "They did take the cart a few blocks away before they dumped it out of the truck by the side of the road. Lee Upton came across it before Corry found it and saw a good opportunity to implicate the homeless man. Lee is the one who planted the evidence in Corry's cart."

"The body hadn't been found yet," the sheriff protested.

"It was their insurance policy," Ray answered. "When it turned out that Corry was the one who discovered the body, the killers thought they had really lucked out."

Ned Toms tamped down coals in his pipe. "Why hide the body in the cemetery in the first place?" he asked. "That never did make sense to me."

"Diff guessed that they intended for Heather to be considered a missing person rather than listed as a murder victim. They didn't expect a Corry-type person to come along and try to sleep in the grave house where they hid the body."

"That's true. If Corry hadn't insisted on changing sleeping places every night, it might have been years before we discovered her in there," Downs reflected. "Final question," he said. "How did they get in the cell to kill Corry?"

"If you will remember," Ray answered, "that morning the whole movie company contingent was at police headquarters. We did a little checking and found that Lee Upton had been the still photographer on the set of Orson's lemon movie, *The Locksmith*, where he evidently picked up a little professional knowledge. Besides, those cells are so old they could practically be opened with a coat hanger. The only reason our prisoners don't escape is that the locks can't be reached from inside the cells. Anyone outside the cell, possessing only a little professional knowledge, could easily open the locks on both cells, silently plunge a knife into Corry, and leave."

"Then it's all finally over with most of the questions answered," Holly announced with a searching look at Diff.

Diff did not notice her glance as he was busy writing two notes on his pad which he finished and tore off to give one to Sheriff Downs and the other to Ray.

Ray slowly mouthed the words as he read Diff's note to himself. He sadly crumpled the note before he looked over at his friend. "Do you mean this? I mean, are you serious about what this says?"

Diff nodded.

The sheriff read his note quickly. "Diff wants to know if he is free to leave town now that the investigation is over. Yes, you are free to go wherever and whenever you like, taking with you our thanks."

"His note to me is a resignation from his job at the police station," Ray said. "Of course, I accept your quitting, Diff. What choice do I have? You're free to go whenever you like, but I must say that both Holly and I are interested in where you are going and what your plans are."

Diff shrugged and then cringed when he saw Holly's stunned look. He might have wavered in his resolve except that he really felt that after he'd been gone a week or two, she'd accept the situation and possibly even begin to date a normal man. He stood up with the knowledge that all he had to do now was go down the steps, cross the yard, and climb into his truck. In ten minutes he'd be on the highway, and the town of Morgan would only be a memory.

He walked across the porch to solemnly shake the sheriff's and Ned Toms's hands. When he went to repeat the gesture with Ray, the police chief threw his arms around him. "I know you've got to do what you think best," Ray said. "But I'm going to miss you around here and really wish things could have been different."

Diff nodded in agreement for there was nothing in the world he wanted more than for things to have been different. He turned from Ray to lean over and kiss Holly on the forehead. When her eyes pooled with tears, she made no attempt to brush away them away until they brimmed her eyes and ran down her face. Her fingers lingered on his arm.

He quickly turned away and strode down the steps and across the yard.

"I love you, Diff James!" Holly called after him. "I love

you, not like a sister or a friend, but as a woman."

Diff stopped midway down the drive and slowly turned. Their eyes met across the yard. His mouth opened as he cleared his throat. "I love you too," he said as his first spoken words in twenty years.

Holly ran down the porch steps, across the yard, and into his arms.